SETH ROW

Teresa Meyerhoeffer Christensen

ISBN -13: 978-0-692-09033-6

ISBN-10: 0-692-09033-9

Bridge2Worlds Books
5942 Harvest Point Circle
Mountain Green, Utah 84050

Dedicated to all those with an open heart and mind who are willing to see things they cannot see with physical eyes. May we all look harder...

PROLOGUE

Amos Applebaum, also known as "Preacher", sat heavily on the well-worn wooden chair. His once intense fight and flight instincts had dissipated some time ago. He was utterly resigned to his unfortunate fate and had even made peace with it.

His nickname had been bestowed upon him by fellow inmates after Amos began using his one hour of allotted yard time to share his new-found faith. Amos had been "born again" and spent isolated long hours in his cell making personalized proselytizing tracks to pass out to his peers, at first on his napkins and later on the sheets of paper the prison provided him. Admittedly, everyone originally saw his finding-religion as a Hail Mary attempt to get out of his death sentence, but either Amos was taking his charade to the grave or he really was converted.

"Amos, the public wants to know what is in your bag of belongings confiscated by the guards when you entered this prison twelve years ago and what you plan to do with each item or whom are you bequeathing them to?" the popular TV, internet, radio host and moderator of Amos's last interview on earth, inquired of the man in orange before him.

Amos looked at the meager, mostly worthless pile of all he had in the world, splayed out on the table between them. He really did not have much of value, but even the great prophets were called to preach without purse or script. He picked up and gently held each item, one at a time, in his hand as he unveiled their futures.

"Well, the cigs aren't much good anymore and I'm no longer smokin', don't want to go into the next life with that addiction. Guess one of the guards can have 'em or prob'bly just toss in the trash," answered Amos as he set the dried out, crunched pack of Camels off to the side.

"Even the oddest items fetch a price for Death Row memorabilia Amos, you might leave them to someone you care about for some quick cash at least, just a thought." interjected the handsome, young, but seasoned, male host.

"I guess so, but don't want anyone I care about to start puffing on them." A sad melancholy permeated his practical words. Like the tobacco had been Amos's worst vice. He next picked up a slightly-misshapen, plain gold band and palmed it tenderly.

"My weddin' ring doesn't stand for nothin' anymore, but I want my son Bucky to have it. He can wear it to remember his pop always loved him and still will whe'ever I end up. Or he can pawn it in a pinch I s'pose."

A single tear trickled down the grizzled cheek and Seth motioned for the camera to pull in for a closer shot. The tear was pure gold for his ratings. This episode would be in the top ten network shows this week for sure. Their viewing audience lapped up this kind of raw emotion portrayed on screen.

The remainder of his long sequestered treasures consisted of pocket change, amounting to a few bucks, and the clothes he was wearing during in-take processing. Amos wanted them distributed to the street people in his old neighborhood. Although a murderer, he had a soft heart it appeared. How much of this display was for the camera and how much he had really changed, Seth was not sure, but Amos did seem sincere and what did he have to gain at this point with an altruistic act?

They went through a few more of the usual questions, interspersed with specific ones directed at Amos from Seth's Monday radio listening crowd. Then he ended the interview with the same question he did on each episode of Seth Row.

"Amos, would you now please take a few moments to share any regrets you may have and end with your last words to the world?"

Amos knew this was coming, Seth had prepped him for weeks, but it did not look like he had prepared anything to say. He did not pull out a crib sheet with written words or composed thoughts on it, he just spoke from his apparently humbled heart. This could go either way…badly if the inmate froze up with nothing to say, or add the element of a mesmerizing last minute surprise due to unplanned words rolling off a condemned man's tongue. Seth leaned in a little closer to his guest. There was no barrier between them and he really was interested in what a nearly dead man had to share.

"First, I want to say I'm so so sorry to her family for what I done. I would never have done it, if I hadn't been higher than a kite on meth and would take it all back if I could. But I can't, so it's prob'bly best that I'm kilt too. Maybe I cun tell Mary I'm sorry to her pretty face, if I get to see her on the other side. May God forgive me for my sins…(brief pause for composure)… like he did that sinner on the cross beside him on Calvary. They wouldn't let me be crucified, but hopefully dyin', like that girl did, will help get me to heav'n. I'm a changed man going to meet my Maker…" Amos completely choked up and could not continue.

The director motioned for the cameras to slowly put back and fade to black.

"And it's wrap", Seth indicated with his hand as the words simultaneously came out of his mouth. This episode would air late Friday night, to ensure a primarily adult audience, on NBC at 10:00 PM…the night before Preacher's 10:00 AM date with death.

CHAPTER 1

Capital punishment is a legal penalty in the United States and is currently used by 31 states and the federal government. Its existence can be traced to the beginning of the American colonies. The United States is the only Western country currently applying the death penalty and one of 58 countries worldwide retaining it. Other industrialized and developed nations that apply the death penalty are Japan, Singapore and Malaysia. South Korea has a law for the death penalty, but has declared a moratorium on executions. The U.S. was the first to develop lethal injection as a method of execution, which has since been adopted by five other countries.

Seth Hoffer was a household word or at least name. His face or voice was broadcast on multi-media outlets all around the country several times a week.

Mondays from noon to three o'clock Eastern Time his syndicated radio talk show "Seth Row Radio" aired all across the United States. His listening audience could call in to chat about and share their feelings on crime in U.S., prisons, punishments, including the death penalty, and even suggest possible questions for his inmate interviews scheduled later in the week.

On Thursdays from noon to two o'clock Eastern and rebroadcast again from ten P.M. to midnight that same day was his Internet talk show "Seth Row…from Death Row" where he had a steady stream of correctional facility "guests" that he interviewed to deduce their thoughts and perspectives on today's prison life. Here he pulled back a curtain to unlock an alternate world to those who watched. His interviewees included wardens, guards, short-timers and life-sentenced inmates, along with those living out their last days on death row.

He also produced special editions of "Seth Row Specials". These shows were broadcast over network TV on Friday nights, only on the weeks there was an execution scheduled in the good 'ole state of Texas. Seth had moved his blooming broadcasting empire to Dallas to "capitalize", pun intended he always added, on the Lone Star state's penal policies, especially its death penalty laws.

Seth graduated with journalism and communications degrees in college, also earning minors in both criminology and social work. He was not sure what kind of career he would eventually do with this unique skill set, but he found the subjects interesting and appealing. He loved learning, so kept attending the university until he found his niche. Turns out his background made him uniquely tailor-made for his current profession.

Several years ago he read an article about the controversial execution of a man with an IQ hovering around seventy. He had committed crimes of larceny, arson and eventually aggravated murder, all while just trying to get a midnight snack from a convenience store that was inconveniently closing at the time. So many thoughts came to Seth's fertile mind.

How could this happen? Was he an evil man or was it an unfortunate turn of events that escalated? What about his family? Was he on his own or did this affect a wife, a child, or a long-suffering mother?

If Seth had so many questions, he reasoned many other people might as well. Modern news outlets liked to focus on the macabre and shocking parts of the story, but few gave a glimpse of who the criminals really were...what caused them to get to the point of carnage.

Seth decided he had something fresh to flesh out and add to an old topic. He would not focus on the heinous acts that placed these corrupted humans on death row, but rather their backstories. The man behind the crime...their life, loves, interests, regrets, and beliefs about life after death. He would humanize the villains. Not in an attempt to exonerate their awful acts or give them fame, but to open the outer layer and see what made them tick. His favorite stories had always been those where each character was multifaceted. The heroes were not always all good and the antagonists not all bad. Mankind he felt was constantly battling the natural-man inside themselves. Seth believed there is good and bad in every person. It just depended on the wolf they decided to feed.

When he finally shared his new-found career path with the person in his life that he was closest too, his mother Marion, she was less-than thrilled. It had been just the two of them while he was growing up. His father, or sperm donor as he preferred to call him, was a shadowy figure that had not really been a part of Seth's life since he was two.

He knew his parents had been married, or assumed so since his mother was a religious woman practicing the laws of Judeo-Christian religion, but there had never been any custody battles, child support or summer visits with dear old dad. He had received birthday cards until he was ten, with a dollar inside for each year he had lived at the current celebratory point. But either ten was his dad's financial or love limit, or he had lost interest, because from that point on, Sam seemed to have dropped off the face of the earth.

Not that Seth had aggressively looked for him either. Maybe it was mutual avoidance. He did often wonder if his father ever tuned in to see any of his programs. Perhaps he did not even know his son had become a success.

Seth was no longer using the surname "Brogan" that he was given by this Irish father at birth. His dad had been so proud that their family name traced back to Saint Brogan, who was supposedly Saint Patrick's nephew and scribe. In reality, a leprechaun family-line seemed more to fit his father than a saint's. Seth had legally taken on his mother's maiden name of "Hoffer" in college.

Marion filed for abandonment before Seth became a teen and a year later returned to her given name at birth. Seth finally followed suit a decade later. He had not changed his face, nor made any attempts to hide his location or identity. The fact was, if his father had any interest in connecting he could. Marion had been both mother and father to him, so she deserved to have him carry her moniker.

He also inherited from his mother Marion his unique moral code, which was definitely unusual for his chosen profession. Seth believed in the Ten Commandments including the sixth…Thou shalt not kill. But he also felt if a person had taken another's life, perhaps their only redemption might come through forfeiting up their own.

He did not believe death was the end, but a gateway to a better place and it was best to arrive there with a clean ticket of entrance. Not only a tooth for a tooth, but a life for a life when it was justified. The death penalty may actually be giving those who had offended God a chance. He was not there to rescue them from their fate, but perhaps help the transition have some meaning.

Working with those preparing to pass on to the other side as they traveled down the road called "Death Row" was a fascinating trek and he enjoyed giving others a glimpse into the journey.

The worst part of the job was the effect it had on his relationships with the opposite sex, all of them except his mother that is. Seth had major difficulty keeping female companionship for any extended period of time due to the darkness of his career.

Seth liked women and considered himself a catch in many areas, not in an arrogant way. He was roguishly good-looking, if he did say so himself. Not exactly tall, dark and handsome, but taller, darkish and TV-screen worthy. Seth stood six-foot even, with wavy, medium-brown hair and piercing, pale green eyes. He could grow a goatee, but preferred to wear his facial hair with a few-day's growth or stubble. He was physically fit and more than financially stable.

However the women he met, those that attracted him anyway, all eventually articulated with various verbiage that his hanging out near the abyss of death rubbed off on him. Seth was often the last person to really speak with the death row inmates before they exited this world. The women in his life felt that the ghosts of his interviewees at times followed him home and swirled around his life. It could be possible he supposed. But he had yet to meet anyone worth giving up the show he had worked so hard to create. He was only thirty-two years old. He still had some time… he was not the one living out numbered days on death row.

CHAPTER 2

Over the forty year period from 1976 to January 1, 2017 in the United States, 1,442 executions were carried out. 1,267 were by lethal injection, 158 by electrocution, 11 by gas inhalation, 3 by hanging, and 3 by firing squad. The number of executions rose at a near-continuous pace until 1999, when they peaked at 98. After that year, the number of executions lowered nearly every year, and the 20 executions in 2016 were the fewest since 1991.

Seth was almost always the first person to arrive at their offices, which were not just offices, but included a sound booth for the radio show and set where they shot some of the non-prison footage for the internet and TV shows. He loved the early morning quiet time to clear his head and think before the noisy, testosterone-fueled, herd joined him. He had been lucky to fine an old vacant studio for extremely cheap rent per square foot. Commercial real estate was fairly inexpensive in Waxahachie, Texas, just south of Dallas, and their frequent destination, the Huntsville Prison, was only two hours more to the southeast.

He first considered locating Seth Row Enterprises in Houston which was only an hour to the south of Huntsville Prison, but the building and business costs were enough higher in Houston to make the extra hour drive from the Dallas area worth it. Besides, being a few hours inland also kept his business safer, more miles removed from the heart of the hurricanes and floods that at times battered the Gulf of Mexico coastline.

And lastly, he definitely did not want to live nearer the prison. Seth felt the crass saying about 'not eating where you defecate' was appropriate in this case or basically the same principle. He did not want to eat, nor sleep, next to the place he interviewed inmates. He would end up sleeping with one eye open, if he slept at all in their vicinity.

Dallas was only thirty minutes north of Waxahachie when he needed city life. He found Dallas was not only a cheaper city in which to live, but had better public transportation than Houston as well.

When they first began this creative business venture, he and his buddy, Bear, had moved to an apartment in downtown Dallas amidst the 'happening' night-life of the southern city. Bear still dwelt there, but now with someone softer, more attractive and without whiskers, Ainsley.

Seth found an apartment nearer their work quarters in Waxahachie. His apartment building was on the

National Registry of Historic Places in the historic downtown next to The Rogers Hotel.

In years past, Waxahachie was a popular place to film in the movie industry. Over thirty movies used it as a backdrop, including *Tender Mercies*, for which Robert Duvall won an Academy Award for Best Actor in the film; *Places in the Heart* starring Sally Field who won the Academy Award for Best Actress for her part; and *The Trip to Bountiful* starring Geraldine Page who also won the Best Actress Academy Award for her role, all in the mid 80's. Seth hoped it may be a lucky-charm location for the success of his shows too and so far he had been right in the assumption.

Also filmed in Waxahachie were scenes from both the television series Walker Texas Ranger starring Chuck Norris and Prison Break. He wouldn't mind the association with Chuck Norris and the Texas Rangers, but was certainly hoping Prison Break was no omen for the future in the work he did. Seth was at home in the more rural and slower paced world of Waxahachie. His mother recently relocated to this suburban Texas town to be nearer her only child and her 'future grandchildren', that he was regularly reminded he had yet to produce for her.

Marion retired from her thirty-five years as a home-economics teacher with a small pension for income. She found due to their lack of teachers, substituting jobs were plentiful here in Texas, so she was able to pick up plenty of extra spending money. She never asked Seth for his help, although he would have been happy to give it. It was, for the most part, comforting for Seth to have his biggest cheerleader close. Waxahachie had become home.

The front door opened to emit a ray of bright sunshine followed by big, burly, Bear Buckley. Bear was Seth's partner and best friend for as long as he could remember. Bear filled out his name well at six-foot four-inches tall and carrying two-hundred and twenty solid pounds without any flab. His golden locks gleamed angelically with the light shining through them and his blue eyes were full of anticipation.

"What's on the docket for today boss?" Bear boomed before the door even had time to close behind him.

"Pull up a chair big guy and let's talk about it. I was thinking about maybe making a run to Huntsville and shooting some clips of the bad boys there if you have enough time today." Seth's voice sounded as Bears eyes adjusted to the lesser light.

Bear was Seth's go-to-guy for pretty much everything. Born Bartholomew Buckley, Bear got his nickname playing football in high school when he would wrap the other team's offensive in a bear hug before bringing them down in a fierce tackle. After high school he and Seth continued on to college together. Bear played linebacker for the Husky's during his first four years and then stayed to finish his degree while Seth kept acquiring more majors.

The boys, who had grown to men together, also started this business together. It was Seth's idea, but Bear as always went along for the ride and pedaled just as hard to make it go. Seth produced and starred in the shows, but Bear directed the episodes, ran the camera team and supervised the editing afterward. They had a blast living together during their college days and then in downtown Dallas when they began this inmate-based-enterprise. Now they were grown up enough to have separate apartments and more separate lives. They still worked together well and had each other's back when needed.

Bear was much better at lasting relationships and had been with Ainsley long enough that they were talking marriage. The two had met at a Dallas Cowboy's game a few years ago. Ainsley was a Cowboy cheerleader and caught Bear's eye before she captured his heart. Bear liked to say they had football in common and the game had brought them together. Seth was not sure that was what sealed the deal, he personally liked football too. But Bear was now Ainsley's 'Teddy Bear'....which was a tad nauseating to Seth. Seth thought Ainsley was great, but missed his more grizzly-Bear friend at times.

"Who's next on the Row's dance with death...let's see...looks like Roy 'the Man-Boy' Manchester. Can we get in to see him and shoot a few takes today? I don't have anything planned later. Ainsley is out of town on a girl's get-away for a friend who's getting married. You know, bridesmaid's thing." Bear shared, like Seth was familiar with bridesmaid's duties.

"Well Brother Bear, sounds like the pressure to 'put a ring on it' is going up a notch my friend. So sorry. Maybe a trip inside the walls will take your mind off your other duties. The warden said we were welcome any afternoon this week to stop by for a shoot. He is even willing to give us a few words of his own if we can fit them in somewhere." Seth was already gathering paperwork they could discuss on the drive down.

He and Bear usually drove together and could handle much of their business on the way, while the camera and sound team took the van with all the equipment they needed. Each of their employees had been severely vetted to pass the stringent clearance needed, enabling them to gain entrance into a maximum security federal prison.

There were no ex-cons on their lily-white crew, not in reference to skin color, but in the clean reputation they required. There could not be even an unpaid parking ticket in their backgrounds if they wanted to work inside the fence. It was interesting enough work so Seth and Bear had been able to snag a few guys who were quite talented in the business, reliable enough to count on and even enjoyed their salty company to boot. Jake, Joey and Gun ran the main camera, back-up camera and sound in that order. Gun had to have extra vetting due to his unfortunate nickname, which had nothing to do with rifles, pistols, shotguns or semi-automatics.

Gun's name and experience had been bestowed in the military, although not for being a crack shot. After he enlisted, the army discovered Gun was a sound technician and had operated sound boards for musicals, concerts and various shows in high school as well as for community events back home. The officers assigned Gun to use his skills helping with the United Service Organization's productions, now known as the Armed Forces Entertainment. Gun had joined up in a wave of patriotism and was okay with any assignment. Instead of shooting the enemy, he aimed music at his fellow servicemen. Gun's name was ironic, since the triggers he pulled did not dispense ammo, but spouted volume.

It was an honor and gave Gun excellent experience in the industry. The USO had a tradition of supporting and increasing the moral in the military since 1941. Their tours performed over twelve-thousand shows a year, to over five-hundred-thousand personnel, at three-hundred and fifty-five installations. Gun had been working with the organization for five years when he retired from the military. He had grown quite comfortable working with men in tense situations wearing uniforms, when Seth Row picked him up.

Jake and Joey had been a camera team since shortly after college. They met and were hired for their first real pay checks right out of school, employed together on a TV shopping channel's set. The show was neither of their dream job, but they gained good experience.

Their most recent gig prior to Seth Row was on a cable television network filming for a political news syndication. After working for several years surrounded by politicians and the whole D.C. crew, Jake and Joey felt death row and prison would be less stressful and more up-lifting. They added a sense of humor and mad skills to the team. All three men were ultimate professionals and got the job done.

The crew were all gathered by ten o'clock and began the two vehicle caravan trek down Interstate 45 south to Huntsville. I-45 was a well-traveled highway for the team, cutting through plain vistas of tiny Texas towns and flat bare land. The booming metropolis of Buffalo marked the half-way point of the journey, should anyone need to stop for a soda or to relieve themselves. Most of the time they could make the uneventful journey without pulling over.

Over ninety percent of the drive was spent discussing their plan of action for the day once they arrived at the Penitentiary, but that still left a small percentage of the time for a quick life catch-up and friend check-in.

"Tell me about your latest damsel in distress these days Seth. What is new in your world of weird women?" Bear teased. They both were well aware of Seth's lack of finesse with females.

"Come on Beary-boy, you know they are not all that bad. I have had a few good runs that almost worked. All women cannot be Ainsley's."

"Okay my friend, let me be more specific. How is prissy Miss Tillie these days and is Junie Blue still blue over you or back in the picture? Are you seeing any long-term potential with either?"

"Women are harder to work with than inmates. I cannot seem to find the right fit. Junie and I are in the friend-zone now, not the kind with benefits. Just pals. She does still appear to care about me because she keeps sending these psych-people to help rid me of the 'ghosts' that she swears dwell with me."

"Does feel a little crowded in your ancient apartment at times my friend. Your pad gives even a big guy like me the creeps. Good for Junie-bee. What about the other?"

"Yah, I suppose Tillie and I are still giving it a go." Seth answered in monotone.

"You sound so excited. I am sure your enthusiasm makes her swoon."

"Bear, she just hates my job and keeps leaving postings for other jobs at my place. It is exhausting. I probably need to get my key back."

"Now that move certainly says 'I want you in my life'! If you need any help from the Love Doctor, just let me know." Bear laughed. "I can have them eating out of the palm of your hand."

"That is not a pretty visual. Maybe if they were behind bars I could relate better."

The two rode side by side in silence for the last few miles. Just after noon the convoy pulled up in front of the old red brick building nicknamed "Walls Unit" because of the red brick walls which also surrounded it. The Texas State Penitentiary was situated on a sprawling fifty-four acres of dirt, cement and grass. Its cell doors had first opened, then shut, to welcome their illustrious clientele clear back in 1849, making this facility the oldest Texas State Prison. It was also the one that housed the state's execution chamber. The Walls Unit had earned the honor of being the most active execution chamber in the United States. Quite the ominous fact to be proud of.

After passing through several layers of security, Seth and team were led into a holding room to set up for the few interviews they would be allowed. On a good day they might speak with six or seven prison personnel, from guards to inmates, on a non-productive day maybe two. Today they were here to focus on Roy Manchester, often called 'Man-Boy' Manchester in the press and prison yard.

His belittling nickname flowed naturally because of his smooth, boyish face that appeared unable to grow facial hair. On the outside, Roy had been heavily into body building and still exhibited some signs of his former glory days' steroid-induced size and muscly physic. He used his yard time to pump iron and maintain his mass. Man-Boy strutted around his hulk-like body with an angry, but baby's-butt smooth, little-boy looking mug on his shoulders. The time back in his cell was spent writing massive amounts of letters to his female fans enlisting them to carry on the causes that ultimately put him behind bars.

Bear and the boys had the lighting and cameras in place, about ready to go, when Warden Walker ambled in. "Hey ya'll want any words from the man in charge here before we bring in the prisoner?"

Bear turned to Seth as he spoke, "Sure Warden that would be great. The cameras are running, just share anything you think might be of interest to those outside these walls."

Walker puffed out his barrel chest as he opened his mustached mouth, "Mr. Manchester has been served well by the state of Texas behind these walls. All will soon see he has been well fed and is physically fit. His mind has also been tended to as he has continued to correspond daily with the outside world. The good people of Texas should sleep safer at night knowing he is here. If we thought he had any chance for rehabilitation we would not be recommending his execution, but Roy Manchester is not a changed man. He will leave this world as violent as the day he arrived at our door. Praise the justice system…that's all…cut….stop the cameras…. How did I sound?"

"You gave us just what we need Warden. Thank you. Let's get a few words from the main guard assigned to his area next if we could." Bear directed as Seth organized his thoughts for Roy's clips.

Mel Miller stepped forward, his gray uniform bulging buttons over a stab-resistant vest.

"Mr. Miller could you share a few thoughts about your time working with Roy Manchester?"

"Man-Boy, I mean Roy, is a tough guy, but always makes me think. He is really smart and knows a lot about a lot of things. He is a big guy, huge really, but he's never tried to push me around. He yells a lot and always wants everyone to know more about the stuff he cares about. There is a lot of stuff he cares a lot about. I started reading up on some of 'em. Like if chemicals are put in our water by the government and if all that fracking for oil is going to cause earthquakes and explosions and stuff. Makes a man think. Roy even knows about politics. He is smart."

"Would you say you like the man?" Seth questioned, refraining from adding the 'boy' to his name.

"Not sure about liking him, not like I'd want to get a beer with him or anything, but I sort of respect him." Mel mumbled.

"Thank you Mr. Miller, you can tell them to bring in Roy Manchester now." Bear suggested.

Roy 'Man-Boy' Manchester was a self-professed cop killer, condemned to death after a jury of his peers found him guilty with no remorse for his crime. He would do it again if given the chance. Roy, probably amplified from the 'roid rage, had been and still seemed to be, a very irate and continually irritated man, who protested pretty much everything when he lived on the outside. Like a mercenary is a soldier for hire, Roy Manchester was a protestor for hire who brought his angst in full force to every job. A guard escorted the convict into the space that suddenly seemed to shrink smaller.

"Hey Roy, this is not our final shoot, but we wanted to get some preliminary background info before your big day if that is okay? Just kind of a relaxed warm up." Seth casually opened.

Jake had the main camera focused on this caricature of a man, while Joey was taking in everything else in the room for cut-away edits. Gun had a mic hanging from the ceiling to catch all the sound and adjusted the lights for best effect. They were hoping for an Emmy nomination this year for their work, so paid every attention to detail.

"Whatever." Roy droned.

"We spoke with Trudy earlier in the week…"

"Why would you talk to that bimbo," Roy interrupted, "She never stayed with me a minute after I was arrested. I know she is hot and probably looks rockin' on camera, but Brenda is my wife now and that is who you should be talking to. Brenda has a brain. She knows me and what is important to me and plans to carry on my work."

"And what work would that be Roy?

"My causes…there are too many to name, but our world is being destroyed on many levels and no one seems to care!" Manchester was starting to get riled.

"Let's talk a little more about Brenda." Seth steered back to a safer topic. "Tell us a little about your love story?"

"Well, when Trudy, that tramp, dumped me, I started answering letters from many women all around the world. I am famous you know and women like a man who takes care of himself and cares about the big issues in the world. Out of all those that wrote me, Brenda got me the most, our letters were passion on the page. She wants to carry on my work and my name when I go to the grave and would carry my baby, if they would give me a chance to make one in here. They did allow us a sterile marriage ceremony, but no honeymoon…haha." Man-Boy shared sarcastically.

"Sounds like quite a woman Roy. We will definitely put some footage of her in the final show. I would also suggest you compose some final thoughts that you would like to leave with the world as well. You will have the chance for a few minutes on the grandstand when you say goodbye."

"I don't have anything else I want to say right now. Take me back. I'm done here. I have more important things to do."

"Sure you do." Muttered Joey, as Mel Miller led Roy the Man-Boy from the room.

They had been in the muggy room for over two hours and none of them minded the abrupt wrap up.

"Let's get some shots of the workout area and see if we can catch any inmates that want to share their thoughts on Man-Boy Manchester before we go." Bear told the team before finishing up their prison day and hitting the open road for home.

CHAPTER 3

There were no executions in the United States between 1967 and 1977. In 1972 the U.S. Supreme Court struck down capital punishment statutes as a result of Furman v. Georgia. All death sentences pending at the time were reduced to life imprisonment. Subsequently, a majority of states passed new death penalty laws, and the Supreme Court eventually reaffirmed the legality of capital punishment again in the 1976 case Gregg v. Georgia. Since then, more than 7,800 defendants have been sentenced to death, over 1,400 of them have been executed and more than 2,900 were still on death row in 2016. Additionally, 158 death-row inmates have been exonerated (acquitted, charges dismissed, or pardoned based on evidence of innocence) since 1973.

It was nearly dark by the time Seth stood in front of his apartment door fumbling with his keys. The day had been long, but productive. The best part of each twenty-four hour chunk of time was usually when he arrived home after a day well spent to unwind, but tonight home may not be the refuge he sought. On the door was a business card, "Exorcists et. All...Paranormal Be-gone Specialist" followed by a name and number. Junie B. strikes again.

Junie Blue was the best, but she was more worried about him than she need be. After just one measly object moving across the table with no one pushing it, and oh, he guessed there was that presence she felt standing over the bed when she had taken a nap at his apartment one day. Junie was just a little skittish. Those weren't the only reasons they had broken up, the relationship had other issues. But some sort of chemistry lingered when the main event was over because Junie was still in his life.

Before even opening the door he gave her a quick call, but got her voice mail. "Junie B., it's me Seth, thanks for thinking of me girly. Looks like you have been busy finding exterminators for the formerly-human for me. Not sure I really need them, but will keep the card just in case. We will have to chat. See ya soon."

Hanging up, he opened the door on his sequestered world from days gone by. The apartment was archaic, but had a somewhat classic Victorian feel. Seth rented the place partially furnished, but his few eclectic items added to the bachelor charm. A comfy leather armchair in front of the television was his favorite spot to sit and watch, use his laptop, rest or read. The main view from his living room window was of the uniquely designed Ellis County Courthouse. If any haunting was going on in this neighborhood, it was most likely coming from across the street. That building looked like a perfect place to host a ghost party.

A backup locale for the haunted house party would be the Rogers Hotel next door. The Rogers was famous for memorable guests in its over century old existence. Frank Sinatra and several Chicago White Sox baseball players once walked its halls. Back in the early days, the White Sox did a lot of their spring training there. So they had a swimming pool specifically built in the basement and during that time historical records say a little girl drowned in it. Her death may have led to the hotel's most famous encounter.

The story goes that the owner of the hotel showed up one morning to find the maintenance man locked in his room trembling and scared. The custodian said that there was a man who came up to him dressed in period clothing from the twenties. This man in retro clothing supposedly asked the maintenance worker to follow him and led him down to the basement. Once there, the stranger pointed to where the pool used to be and said, "Very bad things have happened here." At that moment he immediately disappeared into thin air....according to the tale anyway.

Some patrons over the years also reported door handles jiggling with no one on the other side, and an elevator that sometimes takes guests to the basement, no matter which floor they choose. Once while at the Rogers Hotel, a paranormal photographer even snapped a few shots of what seem to be mysterious ghostly orbs and then all of a sudden the battery for his GoPro, a surveillance camera, died along with its backup battery. Some paranormal experts Seth had met theorize that ghosts or spirits can drain the energy from batteries in order to manifest. Who knows?

Seth's apartment building did not have such an infamous history, but some of his associates felt it was just a matter of time, before the spirits he worked with followed him home and made themselves comfortable there as well. Especially Junie, she was the most wigged out and was pretty sure they had already arrived, but other female friends had also mentioned a few things. Even Bear said Seth's place gave him the hebegebes. For some reason the metaphysical manifestations did not bother Seth.

Maybe if he felt a dark presence that would be different, but so far it was like having a dog or pet around. A little someone to keep him company, if they were even really there, and he did not have to feed them or let them out to do their business.

A sheet of paper on the table caught his eye. Not that he kept the place spotless, but he knew he had cleared it off this morning. Walking over, he saw it was yet another job posting, this one for a weather man at a small station in Dallas. Looked like Tillie had paid a visit to the homestead today too.

Matilda Morgan, or Tillie, was a true Southern belle who found his career less than genteel for her upper-crust family. Daddy Morgan was a well-to-do banker and had connections to get Seth into about whatever job Tillie chose for him. Momma Morgan was the consummate Southern socialite.

Like the TV show the Housewives of Beverly Hills, perhaps Seth could create a spinoff show the Socialites of the Deep South with Lula May and her friends. Seth's dabbling in the muddy puddle of the penal system did not sit well with the Morgan's country club crowd. Tillie, Tillie, Tillie. Seth liked her a lot, there was definitely chemistry between them. Maybe not sparks ignited, but some elements from the periodic table mixing for sure and Tillie really wanted a commitment. Seth was aware however, they really had nothing of depth in common. A pretty face ages and bodies eventually sag and what would he have left...her mother? Not an arousing thought. The writing was on the wall with this relationship and the story was a repeated sequel.

Seth grabbed a Coke from the fridge, kicked off his shoes and collapsed into the soft leather recliner.

He liked to check his messages before settling in for the night in case he had missed anything. Just three messages, it was going to be a nice relaxing night hopefully. The first message was from Gun with an idea he wanted to run by Seth on how to get better sound for the radio show next week. The tech team had discussed the idea on the drive home and he wanted Seth to remind him about it next time they were together. His team really was top notch.

Call number two was also business related from a company that thought they had common interests and may consider merging parts of both their businesses together. Not likely, but Seth would talk to Bear and decide together. Since their success, many had wanted to jump on the gravy train.

Lastly was a message from Marion. She just missed him and was checking in on her favorite son. It helped that he was her only son and had no competition for the spot. The women in his life certainly were attentive, but they could be exhausting. He would call his mom back tomorrow earlier in the day and try to catch her if she was not subbing. Tonight he just wanted to veg.

He turned on the TV and caught a few scores from some of his favorite sports teams before watching the end of a murder mystery. This genre had become so predictable and tame after dealing with the real thing on a daily basis. And the news Seth tried to avoid when possible, he did not need downers at the end of the day…maybe he should start a good news network. There was really nothing he was dying to watch on television and he was too tired to binge watch something on Netflix. He shut off all electronics and grabbed a book from the bookcase to take to bed. Seth still liked the feel of paper between his fingers and supposedly screen lights from devices can cause insomnia. There was nothing like Grisham to help his mind coast off.

He flipped on the reading light next to his bed and laying there on the bed stand was another paper out of place. This paper was actually a napkin. Seth, not one to eat in bed, wondered if Tillie had added a nap with snack to her job-opening delivery errand. He scooped up the paper product to toss in the trash when he recognized words on it. Looking closer, it appeared to be a religious message.

He read: Romans 8:28 "And we know that all things work together for good to them that love God, to them who are called according to his purpose."

Whoa, so weird. Tillie wasn't the religious type and perfumed stationary was more her paper of choice. Not likely she left this napkin behind. His mother was a church-goer and scripture-reader, but she had left him a phone message today not mentioning she had dropped by and a napkin at bedside with scripture was not her style either. Did his abode double as a homeless shelter in the afternoons for the locals? The origin of the paper product was baffling.

A shudder went through Seth as he remembered where he had seen those kind of napkin-messages before. Not that long ago he had interviewed a man who made it a hobby of printing out personalized tracts, even on napkins when paper was not available. Perhaps Amos Applebaum had paid Seth a visit or maybe he had moved in? His home really was becoming a revolving door of weirdness from both sides of the life-death curtain.

CHAPTER 4

Death row inmates with an execution warrant may choose to be executed in the following states by various methods at their own request:

* Electrocution in Alabama, Arkansas, Florida, Kentucky, South Carolina, Tennessee and Virginia.

* Gas inhalation in Arizona and California.

* Firing squad in Utah.

* Hanging in Washington.

"And you're on the air…"

"Welcome on another marvelous Monday to the Seth Row Radio Show. Lines are open to call in as always. Today's top topics are…1) let us know any questions you may have for Roy 'Man-Boy' Manchester during his special episode on Friday night and 2) we will also be having a death row debate, so share your thoughts on your position… pro or con."

Bear suggested it might be too bold a stroke to ask America what they thought about the death penalty, he was not sure what that might tap into, but therein lay the adventure. Seth shared a mini-monologue to get the listening gang going and opened up the phones.

"First caller, please tell us your name, where you are from and what you want to share today."

"Hello Seth, so excited to finally get to talk to you! My name is Lindsey and I am from Lubbock, Texas."

"Welcome Lindsey. What's on your mind today?"

"I want to thank you Seth for the work you do in helping the world understand the importance of the death penalty, it is not barbaric, but fair. I think it gives closure to victim's families who have already suffered so much. Not only is it a deterrent to crime, but justice is better served. Our justice system shows more sympathy to criminals than it does victims these days. My only complaint is that sometimes you make the death-rowers look too nice."

"Just doing my job as an investigative reporter Lindsey. So you are totally pro death penalty?"

"I would say so. The new DNA testing and other methods of modern crime scene science can pretty much eliminate almost all uncertainty as to a person's guilt or innocence. If the convicted is guilty of crimes worthy of death, let's do it."

"Okay one for pro. Any nay sayers? Charlie, you are on the air."

"Hey, Charlie from Portland, Oregon here, totally disagree. I think the death penalty is barbaric and violates the 'cruel and unusual' clause in the Bill of Rights. It sends the wrong message. Why kill people who kill people to show killing is wrong. Life in prison is a worse punishment and a more effective deterrent and other European countries would have a more favorable image of America if we stopped."

"Charlie, why do you care what Europeans think about us? If someone killed your family member would you feel differently?

"I know you would be out of a job if the death penalty ended, so of course you don't take me seriously. I would hope I would be able to forgive, if a family member were killed. And I think the United States has an obligation to set an example for the world."

"Appreciate the comments from both Lindsey and Charlie. The debate is on."

The first hour of the show went back and forth with rapid-fire comments alternating between those who were pro and those con. The most unique input was from a guy who felt putting criminals to death allowed them to return to the world in another form depending on what their crime had been. Like in reincarnation, they got to try again, but were marked by their past life. If they had brutally maimed someone they might have the same injury manifested in their new form. Seth was not sure if this caller was pro or con, but crazy comments did keep things interesting. The second hour he asked again if anyone had questions for Man-Boy.

"Yes Seth, Cassie from Schenectady here, I want to know the meaning of the many tattoos that cover his muscles. I know they must be fairly recent because they were not there in his body building days."

"Noted. Thanks Cassie that is a great question. I am sure his body art will help tell his story in living color with illustrations. Next caller?"

"Marion from Waxahachie here. I was wondering Seth, could you ask Mr. Manchester if he ever answered his mother's phone calls or called her back, before he was sent to prison."

Ouch, his staff sure needed to screen the calls better. Or perhaps this was their attempt at humor? He would definitely get Bear back for this one. "Hello Marion. That could be an interesting insight, to find out how connected he was to his parents and family? Might be a good angle, I will see how the interview plays out. Message received, will call you soon funny lady. Thanks for your call. Next?"

"I would prefer not to give my name and my question is not about Roy Manchester, but another prisoner who recently arrived on death row." A man's voice sounding over fifty, came across the air waves into Seth's sound booth.

"Well, this is open mic Monday, so you are welcome to ask about things other than I suggest."

"Thank you. I was hoping to find out about the new minor addressed as merely 'Joshua' in the news. What is his story and why was he sent to Huntsville instead of another prison? I don't think he is from around there."

"Don't have a fact sheet in front of me about this Joshua yet, but will check him out for the next broadcast," Seth mouthed and motioned for his staff to get on it even as he spoke the words of postponement. "Thanks for keeping us on our toes anonymous caller."

Seth fielded a few more phone calls with questions for Man-Boy and comments pro and con about the death penalty before he closed with… "As always America, it has been a pleasure… Seth signing off from the Row, *reminding you to live well and make every day count!"*

Then turning to Bear and the boys. "All right, you guys got me, but just you wait for pay back my friends. It will not be pretty I promise."

"Next time, call your mom back my man." Bear teased.

"Alright, alright, got it. Moving on, what about that new prisoner. Has anyone heard a word about him? It is not like us to be caught completely off guard."

With that swift segue the team moved seamlessly into their post-show wrap up session.

Bear, Joey and Gun shook their heads in negative responses, but Jake said he had heard of a seventeen year old young man who was coming their way after a controversial case in Idaho. The boy had been convicted of a brutal crime against another child and the system did not want to house him anywhere near the location. Huntsville won the lottery to keep this notorious teen until death did they part. Seth did not like the hush-hush surrounding this new phenom nor the sound of the situation. The prisoner would likely show up on their doorstep soon, if he had not already arrived in their backyard.

"Okay let the research begin. Who wants point on this one? I need to bow out a little early boys. Have a dinner in the city with my woman and want to beat rush hour traffic if possible."

"I will follow up on the leads I already have bossman." offered Jake.

"Thanks Jake-man. Let's all keep our ears to the ground on this one. Anything else? Oh, and Gun, I appreciated your sound suggestions, what did everyone think of the changes?

A ripple of… "great, liked 'em, excellent, improvement"…reverberated off the sound walls.

"Nice work all around men, let's put another episode to bed and go enjoy our evening."

And with that Seth was off. He was not one to let a puddle form under him. He jumped in his Honda CRV and headed north to Dallas via I-35 East. Growing up he had dreamed of a Beamer or Mercedes as his wheels. Even though he could now afford a nicer car, the practical part of him raised by a school teacher still took over. Besides he had room to put his some-day dog in the back.

The drive was not too bad yet, but Seth would have preferred to meet at Pop's Burger Stand in Waxahachie or maybe Braum's if she wanted a dairy dessert treat. Tillie was not a burger or ice cream sort of girl. The Palm, Dallas' upscale dining with swanky atmosphere and white linens was more the Morgan way.

He pulled up in front of the restaurant at ten minutes after seven and tossed his keys to a valet so he could sprint in. Tillie hated him to be late and he did not want to start the evening off sour. The tall, luscious blonde was sitting up straight in her chair sipping on the vodka martini she had ordered, just a 'tiny-bit dirty'. There was a touch of a pout on her lips, but he knew that since he was under thirty minutes past his designated arrival time, the pout would not last long.

"I almost ordered for you Seth. You know I detest eating too late. It makes it hard for me to sleep and I am puffy in the morning."

"So sorry tall, blonde and beautiful. Perhaps we should have met in Waxahachie, I got here as fast as I could,

45

promise. But you could have ordered for me Till, I like your surprises and you do look smashing by the way." Seth had always been a fast-talker, but not necessarily a smooth one, especially when it came to women. His mother was not the best practice. As long as he spoke to her at all and told the truth, he was pretty much good.

"I just want tonight to be really special. I have something important to talk about with you." Cooed the striking co-ed bathed in romantic lighting seated across the table from him. Seth knew he was out of his league and was starting to realize he may be in deep trouble tonight.

"I am all ears now, you have my complete and undivided attention." Seth made the grand gesture of turning off his phone while she was watching. That should score major points.

"First, I was wondering if you saw the weatherman job I left for you."

"I did, thank you Till, but not sure I could support you in the manner you have become accustomed to on that part-time salary." Smooth way to dodge that bullet, Seth congratulated himself.

"I wondered that too. So I talked to Daddy and he said he thought he had a position for you at the Bank. It is a great job, with long-term potential and he could teach you all he knows. He wants you to come in and talk with him about the possibility. Just imagine, you could actually escape your undesirable work environment and do something more respectable. " Tillie looked hopeful.

Please, someone, quick, find me a samurai sword, so I can throw myself on it. Seth's thoughts swirled. He could not imagine a worse fate than to earn a living under Daddy-Warbuck's thumb for ten hours every day. His future was looking bleak in Morgan-Land. But out of his mouth came the words… "Please tell your father for me that is extremely generous of him, but I could never take him up on his offer. He would never respect a non-self-made-man for his precious daughter and I could not respect myself either…And you know I happen to enjoy the way I make my living." Whew. Maybe he was smoother than he thought.

The waiter showed up to rescue Seth and they placed their orders. Tillie requested a seafood salad with no cheese, preferably vegan, besides the fish, with the dressing on the side. Seth was hankering for a steak, medium rare, baked potato loaded with sour cream and the house veggies. Even their food had nothing in common he feared. They consumed their dinners with a small amount of small talk. Tillie was not hungry for dessert. That lettuce must have been impressively dense. But she did still have an appetite for other things it seemed.

"Seth, I have been thinking, it is about time for me to spend the night. We have not had a sleep over yet and you know, we have been together for nine months. It seems like time. I packed an overnight bag with lingerie I know you will love."

Seth about choked on his last piece of meat. He wondered if Tillie knew the Heimlich maneuver and was doubtful for some reason. He should have known this was coming again soon, but thought the Roger Morgan job offer had been all the ammo she had in her for one night. He had under-estimated the girl. Matilda sat cross from him smiling sweetly, wearing a clingy white dress that V'ed deeply between just the right places and was sure to be mid-thigh short when she stood up. She always dressed to catch the eye, but this was provocative at its best. He should have been prepared.

"Tillie, we have discussed this. You know my set of standards do not include sleepovers. I want to respect you, like I respect my mother...bad example...I know our relationship is much, much different, but I want it equal in the respect category. Waiting for marriage to live together, makes it all the sweeter."

It was the mantra he had been telling himself since college and sure hoped was true. Seth wanted to really get to know and love a woman without all the physical complications and baggage, before he committed to a forever together. He needed to keep a clear head for the most important decision of his life without his testosterone doing the talking. If he let a woman move in before marriage and decided against it, he may never get her out. The claim would be staked. Besides, he needed a sanctuary.

"Being so old-fashioned is one of the charming things about you Sethy. I am not suggesting moving in, just a little liaison to give you a taste of waking up to Tillie. And you must admit your place could use an occasional woman's touch, if not a full make-over." She was all gooey like she would melt in a puddle on the chair if he didn't scoop her up soon.

Seth had to be careful not to fall under the spell. He could feel himself being sucked in by her long lashes, soft curves and hypnotizing smell. He could swear she was even emitting animal pheromones to arouse and attract. Be strong Seth, shut your eyes and hold your breath if you have to man. Self-talk had carried him through many a sticky situation.

"Oh so tempting Tillie, but I know you love a man of principle. If I let you wrap me around your little finger you would be out the door tomorrow. No, I will stay strong for our future."

"You cannot be serious. Really Seth?"

"Let's just take things slower tonight Tillie and enjoy the ambiance here or stroll around downtown while we digest dinner?" Maybe holding out was part of his allure. He shortly found out it was not. Matilda Morgan was used to getting her own way and was never rejected.

"Fine, just fine buddy-boy, if that is the way you want it," the words came out sharply staccato-ed as she stood abruptly and gathered up her designer purse, "but you are missing out all the way around tonight Mister

Hoffer." The pout was back and the dress was short, Seth noticed as Tillie stormed out of The Palm restaurant, slipping through his palms as well.

CHAPTER 5

Prosecution can seek capital punishment for aggravated murder, the definition of which varies greatly from one state to another. California for example has 22 factors which constitute aggravated murder, while New Hampshire has seven. But some aggravating circumstances are nearly universal among death penalty states, such as robbery-murder, murder involving rape of the victim, and murder of an on-duty police officer. Several states have included child murder to their list of aggravating factors, but the victim's age under which the murder is punishable by death varies between them too. An official commission in California proposed to reduce these factors to five...multiple murders, torture murder, murder of a police officer, murder committed in jail, and murder related to another felony.

It had been a rough week. Tillie was still not talking to him after her dramatic exit on Monday night. Seth had not returned his mother's call yet; he was not ready to explain perhaps another road block or at least detour in the grandkids endeavor. And there was definitely something beyond normal going on in his apartment, whether he wanted to admit it to others or not.

Seth stopped in at the gym to try to work out and disperse some of his emotionally charged mental malaise by attaching it to droplets of sweat that dripped off his body. He had not exercised in far too long and needed an outlet. Swimming laps might also wash away some of his lingering minor miseries or maybe submerging himself at the bottom of the pool for a while and oxygen-depriving then out. But instead he ended with a relaxing hot tub soak and cleansing steam sauna.

He used to attend Wonder-body World regularly. Junie Blue was a Pilates and yoga instructor there, so Seth had semi-ended the gym relationship along with theirs, to prevent awkward encounters. The post-breakup mourning period was appropriately past, so it was probably time to return. But even pumping iron and running a few miles on the treadmill had not rejuvenated or rebooted his psyche completely.

Seth was having trouble focusing on work and his head was not really in this current Seth Row Special. His mind wandered. Pull it together man and do a decent job to finish this show Seth… was his ongoing mental pep talk to self.

"Roy, I have a few questions America is curious about, if you are willing?" They were already over halfway through Roy Manchester's Seth Row Special and final send off. There was much material they still needed to cover and Roy was not making this interview easy.

"Lay them on me and I will decide as we go if they are worth answering. I have my reputation to retain after I am gone."

"Fair enough. We had a caller wanting to know about your body art. Do any of your tattoos have special meaning?"

Roy looked down at his inked body with obvious pride. "They all do. When I was lifting professionally I couldn't have any, we had to oil up for the competitions and tats would distract from the definition. That is the main reason I eventually ended my lifting career. Each of these beauts represent a cause I've worked on or I'm passionate about. See this whale over my pec," Roy flexed the muscle as he spoke and the finned mammal appeared to be swimming. "I worked on saving the whales before I got into pollutants and chemicals, right here, the bottles with skull and cross bones. The guns are for my weapons running days and the X'ed out turban for the terrorists. You get the idea."

"You sure are the poster child for equal opportunity protesting Roy. I see your whole chest, arms and even part of your back is covered. Which is your favorite."

"That would be the only non-protest symbol on me…see my left nipple is also the nose on a woman's face. That Amazon-looking woman is to honor Brenda and the other good women in my life, placed right over my heart. Tough fighters, willing to get their hands dirty if needed for me.

Brenda is the only person, well unofficial person that will be at the execution, besides those (words bleep-out) reporters that have to be in there."

"It is almost a shame to bury all this meaningful artwork isn't is Roy."

"Actually, I have requested to be skinned or stuffed, so my message can be displayed in a museum or at least given to Brenda and my fans or supporters. I want her to have something special when I am gone to remember me by. I don't want to be put under the dirt out in the prison's Captain Joe Byrd Cemetery and have other lame prisoners assigned to tend to my grave. Some of them would probably piss on it or desecrate it in some way. My remains are destined for greater things."

"I sincerely hope you are allowed your unusual request. Any other wishes or maybe a special last meal?"

"I asked for shark meat, to symbolize going down with a fight. But, I guess this is the only prison in the country that doesn't allow last meal requests. Some other inmate screwed that up for the rest of us. We just get what everyone else is eating that day. Hope they serve something decent. Won't be shark though."

"Sorry about that. Well you can at least share your last words for the world to hear, without censorship except bad language, if you would like."

"I don't have much to say. Most of my words are immortalized in my ink and will also be in a book Brenda is having written about my life story. I hope everyone will buy a copy and get to know the real Roy. All proceeds will go to my foundation which will battle for good causes in any form.

I guess my biggest regret is not being able to make a bigger change in the world, due to that dumb cop getting in my way and making me have to kill him. I didn't want to, but I had to get the job done and he was not going to just stand by and let me blow up that chemical plant.

I also wish I was incarcerated in Utah, so I could be shot by a firing squad. I hate needles." (Seth found irony in the fact most with multiple tattoos felt that way about needles.) "Anyway, I know my many pen pals will miss me. Carry on my Man-Boy Mamas. I am sorry I will not be there to lead the charge. Here is a huge goodbye hug."

Roy opened up his arms wide and gathered them towards the center of his body hugging nothing but thin air. His anger evaporating in this uncharacteristically tender last act and his boyish face looked a bit cherubic. Seth almost felt like giving the guy a hug so he would not look so pathetic. This job created odd emotions, especially when witnessing these end of life events. The show would close with the huge air-hug to show the world Man-Boy had a softer side after all. The policeman's wife would not like it, but she got to share her side of the story in a clip that was being be aired along with the rest of the package.

Seth had an unpleasant taste in his mouth. This one felt icky for some reason. How could he make sense of the complexly strange Roy Manchester without showing lenience on his actions? Was everyone who committed a crime a little bit crazy? He would be glad to have this sequence complete. Perhaps Tillie was right. Maybe he should be a banker.

The team did not seem to have any of his reservations as they wrapped up the shoot. Bizarro world played well to an audience and this show was firing on all cylinders from that view point. The camera work was incredible, they even caught a close up of the pectoral swimming whale. The guys were slapping each other on the back as they packed up their gear. The prison was an eerie place to shoot, so not much in the way of backdrop extras were needed to set the mood of the piece.

"Bear, do you feel at all bad about tonight's show? Are we exploiting these men during their very lowest point?"

"Tonight was a weird one, even for us, but I think our intentions are good. We are giving them a chance to share their side of the story and not leave earth in a vacuum. I think they actually enjoy their few minutes of fame and it may make their deaths a little less senseless. Remember they don't have to agree to participate if they don't want to."

"I suppose you are right. Things just felt different tonight. Must be me."

"Is Seth Hoffer becoming a softy? I would trust you to do my own granddad's last words for the world. You are an ethical man. It will edit out all okay. Just wait and see."

For some reason Seth did not feel much better. His mind was still walking down a path of its own when he noticed he had turned the wrong way and ended up in the wrong wing. He had never ventured this far into the inner workings of the penitentiary before and turned to retrace his steps when his attention was pulled towards a prisoner with a small entourage of guards just ahead.

A tall, slender teen was being escorted down the corridor towards death row. Longer-length light brown hair, that would be buzzed off soon, hung in grimy clumps around the resigned face. Due to the minuscule number of prisoners in this peer group, Seth was pretty positive this was Joshua. The boy stopped and turned to look at him. Hollow pools of near-colorless gray eyes absorbed his very essence. A prickly feeling spread over Seth's skin and he wanted to follow the inmate down the corridor to his cell, but that walk was beyond his clearance level. In the stillness Seth heard solemn words coming from the prisoner's back as he continued on...
"Led like a lamb to the slaughter" ...

CHAPTER 6

For a variety of practical reasons, not all prisons offer the option of having a special final meal. The ones that do often set a $40 limit, to dissuade fanciful meals of caviar and lobster on the taxpayers' dime. Statistically speaking, the most common choice of last meal in the United States is a cheeseburger with fries. However, there have been some rather extravagant and downright weird choices. A man named James Edward Smith once requested a lump of dirt, apparently for a voodoo ritual. This was refused—soil is, unsurprisingly, not on the list of approved prison foods. He had yogurt instead. Robert Buell opted for a single black olive in the hope of his corpse sprouting into a tree, while Gerald Lee Mitchell asked for a bag of Jolly Ranchers.

Relief to be nearly home flooded Seth as he walked down the historic hallway, until he turned the corner to see two human figures waiting at his door. One an unfamiliar man, the other his mother.

"Mother dear, so great to see you. Come in of course. Unless you're on a date with this fellow?" Which Seth was pretty positive she wasn't. "Let me see what else is going on here first."

"This man's name is Raul, Seth. Junie Blue sent him to do a psychic read on your haunted apartment, son." Marion introduced.

"My card." Raul bowed with outstretched arm for Seth to take the small rectangle of card-stock.

"Thank you, Mr. Raul. Sorry, it is too late tonight now, but I will definitely give you a call soon to schedule a new time." Seth said as he stuffed the business card into his pocket.

"I wouldn't count on it. You will probably have to call him back, let me give you his number." Marion said with a mischievous smile as she wrote Seth's cell number down for Raul.

"Thank you kind and lovely lady." Raul took his mother's hand and for a moment looked like he was going to kiss it, like in a Gomez and Morticia moment from the old TV show The Adam's Family, but merely gave it a limp shake with another brief bow instead. Then turning to Seth, "Remember when you call, I prefer to work at night, the spirits are more active and easier to read."

"Oh yes, my mother is nothing if not thoughtful. Thanks mom." Even in his exhaustion, Seth picked up there was something going on between these two and wondered how long they had been talking before he arrived. "I will call you, Raul. Thank you for dropping by and I will thank Junie for her constant concern for me. I am actually fairly comfortable with my lightweight roommates…. Amos anyway, if Roy joins us I may feel differently." Seth added under his breath.

With his third shallow bow in about that many minutes, Raul made his exit down the period-themed hall.

"Come on in mom. Sorry I have not gotten back to you."

"No Seth, not tonight, I can see you are utterly exhausted, go in and go to bed. I caught your show earlier and am just worried about you. Why don't you come to Sunday dinner? You can have a good meal and we can talk then. Bring Tillie or come alone, whichever you prefer."

"I am beat. Thanks mom. I promise to be there for dinner Sunday. Five o'clock? Till is a little ticked with me right now, so we will see about that, but it will at least be me. I will let you know."

"Five o'clock works. Get some sleep between now and then Seth. Looks like you could use it."

Marion hugged Seth good-bye and followed Raul's invisible footsteps down the hall. She did worry and was as meddling as any typical mother, but she always had Seth's welfare first and foremost in her inquisitiveness. Seth understood that.

He opened the door to his humble domicile and breathed a sigh of relief. Home Sweet Home. He knew he should get some extra shut eye, but the packet Jake handed him as he left the prison made him far too curious. Seth rationalized he would not be able to sleep anyway, wondering what Jake had uncovered about their new mystery row-mate. So he dropped into his battle worn recliner and slid the sheets of paper out of the eight by eleven manila envelope planning to just skim them for a few minutes.

Enclosed were the transcripts of the court proceedings from Twin Falls County Idaho...Joshua vs. the Prosecution, with Judge Rob Blevins presiding. No last name for the defendant. That was unusual. And the stack of papers between his fingers was not as thick as one might expect for a death penalty case. Which meant it must have been argued and decided fairly quickly.

Court appointed attorneys do not always exert themselves with extra research and witnesses. Looks like the prosecution had the case served up to them on a platter. Joshua had been found holding the lifeless, bloodied victim in his arms. The evidence was about as good as a smoking gun.

From the dialog of the attorneys and witnesses, Seth deduced the majority of what had taken place out in the wild west concerning Joshua's case. Nearly two years previously, twelve year old Jonny Doe who had lived at St. Edwards Catholic School in Twin Falls, Idaho was found dead across the street from the school in the Twin Falls City Park.

The school also included a small home, really an orphanage, for a few of the students that were looked after by the nuns. Orphanages are rare in these days of foster care, but St. Edwards had a small grandfathered-in hold-over home for parentless children from days gone by. Jonny had been abandoned there as a baby...a John Doe...and the name stuck. The sister's reasoned that John had been the most beloved disciple of Christ and this Jonny would also be. So Jonny Doe, the nun's gift from God, had grown up in their care with about a dozen other kids without homes.

Joshua had been a boarded student at the same school, but had run away shortly before the incident. Jonny was one of Josh's best friends in the school, like a kid brother whom he looked after. That was the sister's impressions from their court testimonies.

The prosecution turned the relationship into something much uglier. The boy had been burned, mutilated, physically abused and blood had been coming from more than one orifice when the body was recovered. DNA showed the blood all over Joshua was Jonny's and Jonny had some of Joshua's DNA on him as well.

For two days the prosecution marched witness after witness up onto the stand to share testimony. Most came from one of two categories: they were either civic leaders, concerned for the safety of their community, or parents of other students at St. Edwards. The consensus continued on and on, Joshua was odd, there was something strange about him, he was just not right. One insinuated Joshua must be on the 'spectrum' and at the very least had Asperger's syndrome. Autism was becoming an increasing popular diagnosis in this country it seemed.

Seth learned that Joshua was never allowed to associate with most of the other children or invited to come to their homes. Another witness shared that Joshua spoke like he was from another century and had few friends. The words Seth read made him feel sorry for the kid, but did not prove he was a murderer, just that many of his schoolmates were entitled jerks. Perhaps the young man had finally just flipped out with such a lack of social inclusion. It sounded like they were lucky to not have had a mass school shooting or stabbing, like so many schools on the news these days.

Police Officers Paxton and Muldoon, who were called to the crime scene, told of the gory site they arrived upon. They spoke of the complete calmness of the defendant in spite of his tears. The behavior was atypical of a youth holding a dead body, unless the individual had planned it in the first place. That was purely subjective, not factual. What, no objection there? Was the defense asleep?

Then Officer Truman from the sheriff's department who worked with troubled, misplaced youth, shared insights on children who suffered from failure to form attachments, a condition called privation. He expressed his concern that Joshua's abandonment may have played a part in the crime.

Joshua appeared to be pretty detached from all humanity. The testimonies continued. There was a virtual parade of people pointing the finger at Joshua's guilt.

When the defense finally got a turn, their efforts were woefully lacking. Since Joshua had such a small circle of acquaintances to draw from, their main witnesses were the nun's from St. Edwards Catholic School. Three were put on the stand. The women in flowing black spoke nothing but words of affection and concern about the boy. "Joshua had been with them since he was an infant." "He was a good boy, never a behavior problem." "He was not perfect. He did day dream during some of his classes." "He always did all that was asked of him, in his quiet way and had a gift for the ministry." "His ability to memorize and recite scripture was remarkable."

You would think the jury would find nuns believable. The prosecution countered that they were women of the cloth and of course saw the good in everyone, even the sinners. It was in their nature to forgive. Not much of a defense. No clear explanation as to why Joshua left the school in the first place nor an alternate scenario of why he returned and happened to be with Jonny at the moment of his death was ever given.

Joshua was never put on the stand in his own defense for some reason, possibly due to fact he was under age and also a street urchin with no one to really advise or stand up for him. Maybe his lax lawyer thought he would crumble under pressure.

Joshua's statement to the police after being found sitting in tears, gently cradling the boy in his arms, had been read aloud in court…"I arrived too late to save Jonny, so I held him and talked to him softly until he died. I wanted Jonny to know I was there, that I loved him and that he would be okay where he was going. No one would hurt him anymore. I am not sure who did those horrible things to him. (Sobs from the accused.) There is that county jail across from the other side of the park, maybe someone from there got him? I truly don't know. I love Jonny and would never have hurt him in any way. I wish I could have saved him or stopped whoever did it. I should never have left him." (Too many tears to go on.)

There was also some closing testimony from a 'Father Brogan' who was the priest over St. Edward the Confessor's Parish in Twin Falls which was under the Boise Diocese. The name gave Seth a start. What an odd coincidence. Joshua also had a Father Brogan in his life, but Seth's father Brogan did not seem to be the priest-type. Father Brogan spoke up for both boys from his Parish…the condemned and deceased. But he did not have enough contact, nor enough influence within the system, to help with either it seemed.

The evidence was not in Joshua's favor. Another person of interest for the crime was never really looked for or found. The court believed they had their man. The trial lasted less than a week. The jury was out less than a day. Due to the violence of the crime, age of the victim and public outcry, Honorable Judge Blevins was able to swiftly secure a death penalty sentence, even though Joshua was just now seventeen. He had been only fifteen when the heinous crime took place, but he was convicted as an adult.

The rural farming community in the Magic Valley did not want a young murderer in their midst for one day longer than needed and Texas executed at seventeen. He had been assigned to wait out the end of his short days in the Huntsville Unit. Seth had done more than skim the document. He had read every word. It was after two o'clock A.M. before he finished and he was wide awake now. His body was still hammered, but his mind was circling and digesting what he had just read.

A sound came from the kitchen. Seth thought he heard movement and drug himself out of the chair to see what was going on. Maybe he had mice, or perhaps gigantic rats had time to grow and take up residence in this hundred year old building. He knew his brain was so sleepy he could be hallucinating or hearing things, but he could not just sit, so started inspecting.

At first there wasn't anything he could put his finger or eyeballs on in his tiny cooking area, but Seth felt like something was amiss. It was late and no one was watching he decided to go ahead and ask, "If anyone is here, let me know? Can I help you? If not I need to get some sleep. Thanks."

He scanned the room looking for anything. The countertops looked similar to how he left them and no cupboard doors were ajar. The stove was turned off and the refrigerator was closed.

On the door of the fridge was Seth's collection of magnets from all the places he had traveled to. He and his mom had started it when he was younger. He did not own a steamer trunk or cool leather suitcase to put travel stickers on and he did not have a car at that point to decorate with bumper stickers.

Seth was not sure he would plaster his bumpers even today. He thought stickers looked a little trashy on a car and left a trail not only of places the person had been, but social issues a person supported. Far too much info on display.

Maybe magnets could be considered girly, but they worked as his travelogue. Seth had accumulated about thirty from vacation and work spots around the country and even a couple international locations. The Eiffel Tower and Big Ben were the furthest destinations represented.

Seth was not OCD with them, but kept a semi-pattern across the top and down the left side of the fridge door. Looking closer, it looked like two magnets had been separated out of the line-up and moved over to the right side on their own. The highlighted ones were from two trips to opposite sides of the country, Yosemite Falls and

Niagara Falls. Interesting, did someone have a flowing water fetish?

The symbolized message suddenly hit him. Someone had spelled out or indicated 'two falls', or could they possibly be saying 'Twin Falls', with pictures in his kitchen?

Seth knew it was late and his mind could be taking him to unlikely places. But he had to admit he was a little freaked out. He could call Tillie, but she was already miffed at him, if he interrupted her beauty sleep he may never get off her black list. Junie would probably relish a paranormal phone call in the middle of the night, but it wasn't fair to keep her dangling on the hook at his beck and call, if there was no future for them. He wondered if it was too late to call Bear, but decided to try anyway.

A groggy "Hello?" greeted him on the other end of the line. "Seth this better be an emergency."

"I guess it can wait Brother Bear, I just needed to hear your voice."

"Are, you sure man? Really, what do you need?" Then from further away from the phone. "Bear who is it? Is that Seth?" Sounded like Ainsley was there with him.

"Nah, I got this. Go back to sleep with your girl. Sorry to have interrupted anything."

Seth hung up his phone. In the light of day two magnets being moved would be odd, but not so unsettling. If he had not just read the court case from the same county, he may even be able to walk away unaffected. The line between life and death was getting blurry in his life. Another one of his interviewees would be crossing that line in a few hours and a soul who already had crossed it was communicating in his kitchen. This was going to be a long night. Maybe turning on the TV would engage his mind and take his thoughts away from the real world around him. If you could call it that.

CHAPTER 7

Top three state numbers on death row: California-754, Florida-395, Texas-254. The distribution of death sentences among states is loosely proportional to their populations and murder rates. California, which is the most populous state, has also the largest death row with over 700 inmates. Wyoming, which is the least populous state, has only one condemned man. But executions are more frequent, and happen more quickly after sentencing, in conservative states. Texas, which is the second most populous state of the Union, carried out over 500 executions during the post Furman era, more than a third of the national total. California has carried out only 13 executions during the same period. Collectively, Texas, Oklahoma, and the South accounted for over 87% of U.S. executions in the same period.

Seth slept most of Saturday. Not only had he been up much of the night before, but sleep served as a defense mechanism to avoid letting his mind dwell on what was happening down in Huntsville that morning.

He called Tillie late afternoon, after he had shaken off the daytime sleep. She was still chilly to him, but it was more veiled. Had Seth not known her as well as he did, she may have seemed back to normal. He decided not to invite her to dinner at his mother's. Dealing with one woman at a time was enough. He could use some insight-time from the less needy and more objective older woman in his life. Seth knew his mother's agenda did not usually include buttering him up or manipulating him for any reason, so he could trust her advice.

It was a glorious spring day in east-central Texas. Warm enough to not need a jacket and the humidity had not yet kicked in with moisturizing heat that stuck itself and everything else to the skin. Seth decided to walk the two and a half miles to his mother's small ranch-style home north of downtown where he lived.

Marion attended her non-denominational Christian church until noon and afterward would be home working on dinner much of the afternoon. She went all-out when Seth came over. Marion did not entertain much, but enjoyed cooking for her only child. She was the epitome of a classic Jewish mother who equated food with love, but still somehow maintained her slim figure at nearly sixty.

Seth's mother had been raised in the Midwest on a small farm where her father eked out a living growing corn and raising pigs amid frequent drought conditions. Seth could remember visiting there several times when he was young. Usually in the summer when school was out and his mom was on a break from teaching. Through little boy eyes, his grandparents looked ancient from the first time he remembered meeting them.

Grandpa Marv's skin was a leathery, dark-brown that blended in with the color of the soil after years of working it. The lack of water that plagued the fields he planted, apparently prevented moisture to his face too. His white hair stood up straight from its roots, even after his sweat-stained baseball cap was removed and kind blue-green eyes always looked out at Seth from below his grandpa's hat brim or hair halo. Seth could also picture a tractor he liked to ride, seated in front of his Grandpa on the wide metal seat.

Grandma Ada always had her gray hair pulled back in a twist or bun at the nape of her neck and wore an apron she frequently dried her hands on in his mental memories. She would greet them with a freshly baked pie to eat upon their arrival and made sure they never went hungry the whole time they were there. Grandma Ada's stories that flowed from her lips, filled him even more than her pies to his stomach.

In his memory, it was a quintessential Norman Rockwell painting and life. Rural living had molded his mom into the salt-of-the-earth gal she was today. Maybe she didn't grow crops like the grandparents, but she had raised a pretty decent son all by herself on an educator's salary, which enabled her to be home with him during the summers. For a child having grown up with a single parent, Seth never felt like he missed out. Marion had been there for all of the important moments in his life. He was given all he needed and always felt loved.

Both of Marion's parents were gone now. Her one brother, Stephen, had not wanted to inherit the struggling farm, so sold it to pay off the bills after their parents had passed. He lived up north near Chicago working for an agricultural business that sold farming equipment. His upbringing on the farm had not gone to waste after-all.

Seth didn't know anything about his missing father's parents. His family circle was pretty small, if two people could even form a circle. His mind wandered as he walked.

The traffic was light and Seth cut through side streets and along the green belt as he savored the sunny day. Walking cleared his head and gave him inspiration. Seth felt he was soaking in his religion via the rays of light that pelted his skin. He really should go with his mother to her indoor congregation some Sunday soon. The effort would make her happy. Maybe on Mother's Day. She would appreciate the gesture more than any gift he could buy her.

In the time-verse-things dilemma, time was usually far more meaningful. He wrote the idea on his phone so he would remember to join her on the second Sunday in May. Way to go Seth, got your shopping done early, he congratulated himself. Organized worshipping would probably do him some good as well.

Seth went to church with his mother while growing up for the most part. During high school his attendance had been more sporadic. With no male role model in the home, Seth pushed pretty hard at his adolescent boundaries. He was what one might call a 'conflicted-teen' for a few years. Like most teens who were trying to find out who they were and where they fit.

While in search of the real Seth, he dabbled in sports and theater and was not bad at either. He was also elected one year to serve in student government for his school. He enjoyed being in front of his peers and planning events in their behalf. However, he also wrestled with his darker half at times.

Marion was called to the principal's office on more than one occasion to hear tales of his now regrettable escapades.

Once Seth was suspended for dropping his pants in history class on a dare. He did not bare himself to all-natural, but had been wearing some pretty appropriate boxer shorts beneath his tastefully tattered jeans. The girls in his school could walk around the halls wearing much less it seemed, such a double standard, but he humbly paid the price for his antics. There was even a hazing incident involving some of the underclassmen which he was not proud of. It might be called bullying today.

Through all Seth's angst and self-discovery, as he attempted to figure out which wolf to feed, Marion had been there. Seth was sure it must have been embarrassing for a teacher to have her own child be the source of administration's concerns. But his mother never made him feel like dirt, when she definitely could have. She let him know she believed in him and saw the good boy (now man) inside, even when he fought to find the Seth she saw and was not as sure he could.

About halfway to his mother's house Seth noticed a mangy looking dog started following him. It was one of those if you saw it at the pound you would feel sorry for it, but never take it home. The breed was not recognizable. He or she, it looked like a he, was medium-sized with a thin, scraggly, straight, once-white coat. Mongrel variety, if he had to identify it. The beast did not seem too ferocious, so Seth let the dog join his Sabbath stroll.

They both arrived at the designated destination on Wildflower Way shortly before five o'clock and could smell the dinner cooking from outside on the porch. The dog cocked his head hopefully at Seth. "Sorry but this is where we part ways my good man," Seth informed the animal as he opened the front door and walked in.

Marion rushed forth to greet her son with a warm, welcoming embrace. He could see across the small expanse the table spread before him with beef stroganoff over thick homemade-style noodles, one of his favorites. The main dish was surrounded by garlic green beans, a green salad topped with berries and nuts, warm rolls and raspberry freezer jam. His saliva started juicing just looking at it.

Seth felt a pang of guilt thinking about the thin dog shut outside this feast.

"Looks wonderful mom, almost too good to eat." Seth thanked.

"And I made the fresh peach pie you love for dessert."

"Pulling out all the stops today Ma. What is the occasion?"

"Just happy you are here." Marion admitted.

Seth wasn't sure he had looked at, or at least really seen, his mother for a long time. He still saw a tall smiling woman with a kind, gentle face, but now noticed lines had crept in when he was unaware, creasing and crisscrossing that face. Lids drooped over her hazel eyes that had always held love for him. Her hair, which she continued to color the same shade of brown from when she was younger, was sprouting nearly white roots and her once defined figure was growing soft. His ageless mother was getting old. Where had the years gone? He needed to try to make more time with her while he had it.

They sat down to the delicious dinner, said grace over it and began their meal with his mom's routine one-hundred questions for him.

When they got to dessert Seth spoke up, "I actually have two questions for you today mom. Turnabout is fair play you know, my good lady." Seth, emphasizing the first *'you'*, then speaking in a gallant gentleman's voice teased. "But in all seriousness, I respect that life has not always been easy for you and possibly understand why you have avoided talking about dad, or Sam, for most of my life. I'm old enough now, have been for quite a while, and am ready to know more. Could you please paint a picture to help me know him better?"

"I guess it is time and only fair. What do you want to know Seth?"

"Anything and everything. How did you guys meet, why did he leave, even things I don't know to ask. He is a part of me and perhaps has affected my relationships without me even realizing it."

"Well, let's see, where to begin? I met your father when I was a baby, only in high school. We were both juniors and had physical education together. It was the first time I did not dread the class in my academic history. Sam Brogan captured my heart with his wavy blonde locks, which he passed on to you by the way, only in a slightly darker version, also his athletic physic and his on-the-go attitude.

Your mother may have been shallower in her younger years. Sam was quite a hunk. He was fun and I felt safe with him. We dated through the rest of high school and most of college, before making things official. Perhaps before Sam was ready, but we were at that point in a relationship where you move forward or move on…you know 'fish or cut bait.'

We were still young. Sam finished his communications degree, he was a great communicator, you get that from him too, but he had trouble finding a steady job that put his skills to use. You did much better with those skills you were blessed with Seth.

I ended up being the main bread winner and an educator's income is definitely a no-frills budget to live on. When you came along, Sam felt even more pressure to provide. His restless nature became more pronounced. He wanted you to be proud of him and would take random jobs here and there, often out of town. Sam really was a good father. He adored you. But as you know, one day when you were two, he never returned from one of those out of town jobs.

At first I was panicked and thought something awful must have happened to him. Then you started receiving those cards each year near your birthday, until you were ten. I think that was the best he could do, to let you know he still cared and let me know not to worry. The communications never had a return address on them and the post marks were never from the same state. I considered hiring a private investigator, but funds were low and what would that help? Sam hated to be told what to do, I could never and would never force him to return.

When the cards stopped coming, I almost continued them, pretending they were from your father. But you were far too smart, an investigative reporter in the making, and would have seen through my charade. In the long run, I thought it would end up cheapening those he had sent. I haven't heard from him since, but used to occasionally find some anonymous cash in the mail, which I liked to assume came from him. I suppose he could be dead now, but for some reason I don't think so. I feel I would know. He was a good man Seth, always remember that. He just felt like a failure and had trouble facing the life he had, so escaped it. I have never regretted our relationship for a moment.

The best part of my life came from it…you."

Seth felt conflicting emotions, "Do you think there is any possibility Sam might have become a priest?"

"Not likely, Sam liked sex…. stop covering your ears Seth, you said you were old enough to handle this information now… but I suppose stranger things have happened. He was a devote Irish Catholic. Not the kind that went every Sunday, but it was deep in his heart. His parents emigrated from Ireland, during the intense conflicts and clashes in the 1960s between the Catholics and Protestants, to escape the violence. Why would you ask that?"

"No reason yet, just wondering. I came across a Father Brogan in a case I was reading. And for the record, a child is never old enough to discuss what their parents do behind closed doors. I like to believe in immaculate conception under those circumstances. Let's change the subject.

I have another question. Do you believe in supernatural happenings or events, mom?"

"What do you mean exactly, Seth?"

"Do you think spirits who have died can still be around and communicate with us?"

"I do believe in life after death that we continue on in some form even the worst of us. Perhaps we go to a place of peace and learning, always continuing to grow in knowledge. I suppose if a person had unfinished business he might be tied to the earth and not as able to move on. Why do you ask?"

"There have just been some not-easy-to-explain experiences at my apartment. Others have noticed them too. You saw Junie is still sending services to my place to help rid me of the 'presences' that frightened her when we were together. I'm not sure how I feel about lots of things in my life right now. I trust you to give me a straight answer on this mom, what would you do?"

"Go with your gut. You have always had good intuition, follow it. If you feel a dark or concerning presence I would get out, even move. But if the occurrences are just unusual, go with it, perhaps someone is trying to tell you something. You are a good listener. Use your interview skills in this unique avenue to determine if your apartment is just old, thus lending itself to imaginations going wild, or if there truly is something more. You are up to the challenge, I have yet to see you run from one."

"Thanks mom." Marion was a grounding presence in Seth's life. He felt better just voicing his concerns out loud to her. "I guess I better push off if I want to walk home before it gets too dark, know I appreciate you more than you know."

"Love you always and forever....know I am always here for you, my boy."

With affirmations ringing in his ears, Seth headed outside. The dingy dog was still waiting and wagged his tail in anticipation when he saw Seth. Seth poked his head back through the doorway.

"Mom you don't happen to still have a bone from the meat in the trash do you?"

Marion retrieved the steak bone from the stroganoff's beef and handed it to her kind-hearted son, knowing he would never get rid of the pound puppy now.

CHAPTER 8

The last public execution in the U.S. was that of Rainey Bethea in Owensboro, Kentucky, on August 14, 1936. It was the last execution in the nation at which the general public was permitted to attend without any legally imposed restrictions. "Public execution" is a legal phrase, defined by the laws of various states, and carried out by court order. Similar to "public record" or "public meeting," it means that anyone who wants to attend the execution may do so. Around 1890, a political movement developed in the United States to mandate private executions. Several states enacted laws which required executions to be conducted within a "wall" or "enclosure" or to "exclude public view." Most states laws currently use such explicit wording to prohibit public executions, while others do so only by enumerating the only authorized witnesses. But nearly all states allow news reporters to be execution witnesses for information of the general public. Several states also allow victims' families and relatives selected by the prisoner to watch executions. An hour or two before the execution, the condemned is offered religious services and a last meal (except in Texas). The execution of Timothy McVeigh on

June 11, 2001 was witnessed by around 300 people by closed-circuit television. Most were victims' relatives of the Oklahoma City bombing.

Spending Sunday evening at his mother's house had been rejuvenating. Then Monday's radio show with call-in theme "Do You Believe in Life after Death?" went so well, Seth decided to continue the topic on his internet show today. He requested, and the team received, permission to do the live show on site at the prison this week. The replay later tonight would be re-broadcast from their studio back in Waxahachie.

The Row-bots, a nickname Seth had given the team, were interviewing various inmates and guards to share their thoughts about life after death to see who to put on camera. Where the radio callers had been over fifty percent believers, those incarcerated were running less than thirty percent who had any belief in life beyond the grave. All the interviews had to be totally voluntary per prison orders and the warden had eventually given permission to include two from their death row population.

Harold Testerman was next to be executed, so that one had been easy to get permission for. Seth had to work harder to convince the warden to allow Joshua on the show. Walker had insisted that the teen's execution was months away and there could be possible appeals. Seth had reasoned that with a court appointed attorney the likelihood of appeal was slim and that America was quite interested in their juvenile on the row. Finally, Warden Walker had acquiesced and allowed it.

A lifer had just expressed vehement doubts on air that there was anything else after he was snuffed out, he was making the most of the time he had left behind these (bleeped) walls. Mel Miller, who seemed to love to be in front of the camera, was next in line to share his thoughts.

"Hey Seth, good to have you guys here. It's nice to have a diversion and a chance to talk about meaningful things."

"Hello again Mr. Miller, you are becoming somewhat of a regular on our show. Has the time you have spent as a guard here influenced your feelings on life after death in any way?

"Well, not sure I have thought much about that before. Not much of a religious man. I guess I'd like to believe there is something after we go. If not, what is this all for? You know, just being here."

"So what do you think, choose a side my man, yay or nay, and why?

"Yay, I guess. I don't believe we are just nothing afterwards. It seems some inmates maybe stick around here for a while after they are executed. I sometimes think Man-Boy is still here over by the weights some days. I miss that one."

"You feel there may be deceased prisoners still within these walls? No wonder there is overcrowding in America's prisons today, especially if they don't leave when dead." Chuckled Seth.

"Thanks Mel."

"Let's take a quick break guys before taping the last two from the Row. Those guys are knocking on death's door. This should hit close to home for them." Seth suggested. Bear nodded in agreement. He needed a break. They all did.

The team put down their equipment to take a quick stretch as a commercial played over the air.

"What about you guy's thoughts on the subject matter?" Seth asked as he took a swig of his water.

"After hanging out at your house, I agree with Mel Miller, there's got to be something afterward.

You have enough visitors to host an afterlife retreat in your pad. Maybe you should figure out how to charge admission," laughed Bear.

Jake agreed, he was a believer. Gun, was pretty sure there was nothing afterward, but maybe intelligences carried on in some form. And Joey was back and forth debating even with himself, so an undecided vote for him.

Break time was over and Harold Testerman was led into the room.

"I don't want to take away from your last interview Mr. Testerman, but since you are the closest to crossing the great divide, I am curious on your thoughts of what you will find there?"

Harold was not a personality like Roy, Man-Boy, had been. It was obvious he was not at home speaking with the media or probably pretty much anyone. He slouched down on his chair and spoke in a low monotone voice.

"As a scientist it is hard to speculate. I can only say what I know to be true. Experiments by Dr. Duncan MacDougall were done during the 20th century in Haverhill, Massachusetts. He weighed six bodies just moments before and then immediately after dead. It was determined that a body lost approximately three-fourths of an ounce, or twenty-one grams, at the moment of death.

He performed the same test with fifteen dogs who lost no weigh upon death. From that data I would have to determine a human body has a soul or some other essence which leaves upon expiration. As to where that matter goes, I could not say. I have high doubts in the heaven/hell theory, but there are many ways matter could be re-consumed or recycled by the earth."

"Fascinating Mr. Testerman. Are you personally afraid to die?"

"I would prefer to live and continue my work, but as that does not appear an option, I look at death as my last great experiment. I will know definitively what takes place at that moment. It is just unfortunate I will not be able to write a paper for science documenting the facts from a personal perspective. Or if I am able, will have no way to send it back. Perhaps that will be my next endeavor, figuring out communication between dimensions. We will see."

Harold had become profuse. Who knew a chatty man was buried under all that science. Seth wanted to save anything else Harold had to say for the Seth Row Special filming in a few weeks.

"Thank you for sharing your knowledge and insights Mr. Testerman, we look forward to visiting with you again soon."

Only one inmate was left to talk to and this one made Seth uneasy for some reason. Joshua was escorted into the room wearing shackles with his head hanging down. He did not slide into the chair like the others, but preferred to stand, raising his head to look Seth in the eyes.

"Joshua, thank you for speaking with us today. Would you be willing to share with America your beliefs on life after death?"

"Do you believe life continues after death Seth?" Joshua asked in a clear, quiet voice.

"I could not do this job if I didn't. It seems almost immoral or even amoral to dance with those at the door of death if I did not believe it led them to a better place,"

Seth answered before thinking, "hey, are you taking control of the mic here, I asked you first."

"In answer to your question….Once there was a boy born, that those who genetically created him, did not even want. He was abandoned to be raised by others, who were for the most part good, but could not love him as a son. The people who surrounded him became quasi family and they took care of one another the best they could. Most people are basically good, but evil does exist in this world, even pure evil. Good can vanquish evil; light is more powerful than darkness. When a door is opened between two rooms, one full of darkness and the other light, the light overcomes the dark, but that is not always the plan. At times darkness or evil triumphs for a short time in the vast expanse of eternity. Sometimes to escape the evil, one has to cross through a door into pure light. I believe there is a better place, full of pure love and brilliant light, where everyone is cherished as a son or daughter. I believe we do continue on and it is not a transition to be feared….this birth we call death."

Seth was not sure how to answer, he did not want to disrupt the moment, but linger, bathed in the tranquil feeling. After probably too long a pause, "Are you speaking of yourself or of Jonny?"

"I am speaking of all mankind. We are in this together. To help one another on our journey back to the light."

"Thank you for your illuminating insights Joshua. Hopefully you can bring some more light to this dark place while you are here." And since nothing could top what had just been said, Seth closed the show with his trademark, "As always America, it has been a pleasure…Seth signing off from the Row, reminding you to *live well and make every day count!*"

And with that, Joshua returned to his cell and Seth sat wondering what had just transpired. This was not a normal exchange. There was something elevated about the experience that he could not explain. The interview was almost more ethereal with Joshua standing before them in the flesh, than his encounters with the transparent phantoms at his apartment. Joshua was an odd duck, no doubt. Had his abandonment, extreme isolation and religiously focus environment made him a psychopath?

Seth had at least had a mother and public school to balance out his male parental figure's exit. Seth's thoughts continued to follow the strange boy down the cement hall as he turned back to the team.

"Jake, thanks for finding me the transcripts on that one. He intrigues me. If anyone uncovers anything else on this guy, please pass it along. Bear, we've got to dig deeper, I have a feeling there is something everyone has missed here."

Bear and the boys agreed they were all in, then went to pack up the van for the return trip and replay of the show from the studio later that night. As Joey slid open the van door, a zombie-wrapped, undead-appearing actor jumped forward from the back of their truck. More than one of the shocked tech team screamed like a girl. All Seth said was "payback time boys, payback time. I warned you it would be coming." The guys climbed into the vehicles, after their vital signs recovered from Seth's fright-mare payback prank. It had been worth every penny of his two-hundred dollars.

No one talked much on the drive home. Each was pondering and receiving their own level of understanding from the prosaic words they had heard in Huntsville.

When Seth pulled up to his building, the same scraggly dog from Sunday lay lounging on the stoop. Its ears perked up and he stood when he saw Seth arrive. It was as if he had been waiting for the master he had already claimed.

"Well boy, we meet again. You know, I could actually use the company tonight, so come on in. I'm not sure management would be thrilled, but other overnight guests are allowed on my contract. You are probably better behaved than some and I won't mention you have more hair than most. But don't tell Tillie on me okay, she will be jealous for sure."

The dog followed Seth up the stairs like he knew the way and was going home.

"What should I call you? Dog will not do even for a night. Let me think…how about 'Barney'? You are scrawny and comical looking, like Barney Fife, played by the actor Don Knotts in that old black and white Andy Griffith Show set in Mayberry. You can be my deputy dog, Deputy Barney Fife.

How does that sound?"

The new furry Barney Fife at Seth's heels, seemed content with whatever he was called. However, when Seth opened his door and stepped through its old frame, a ridge of hair stood up straight all along Barney's back and he let out some warning barks, hesitating and not entering.

"It's okay Barn. Are you telling me we have unexpected guests again? They won't bother you, maybe you will even grow to be friends. I guess I do need to call Raul back. Now where did I put his card?"

Deputy dog finally came across the threshold, but was still on alert. Seth shut the door and having located the business card for 'Raul's Psychic Readers' pulled out his phone and dialed the number.

"Raul here, ready to unmask your paranormal visitors. How can I be of assistance?"

"Raul, this is Seth, Seth Hoffer, from a week or so ago. Junie Blue sent you to my apartment?"

"Yes, yes, how is your lovely mother?"

"Just dandy, thanks for asking… I think… I am ready to make an appointment for one of your readings now, if you are available."

"Actually, I am booked solid for over a week out, so sorry Mr. Seth. However, I do have a daughter who works with me and she is very good at what we do. I am proud to say she may even surpass her father… one day. Are you willing to work with Halle? If yes, I can schedule her for a reading on Sunday, Monday or Wednesday of next week. We like to work at night, so around nine o'clock?"

"Let's say next Wednesday at nine o'clock. Thank you. Not sure what I really expect her to do, maybe just tell me I am not crazy."

"No worries, Halle will know what to do, she will take care of you. I will send her there next Wednesday."

Seth felt better taking some step forward. Like most things, you first had to admit you had a problem before you could conquer it. He was not even sure he wanted whatever it was gone, but he did want to know what he was dealing with. Hopefully this psychic reader thing was not a hoax. At least he had Deputy Fife at his feet if he needed back up tonight.

CHAPTER 9

Psychologists and lawyers in the United States and elsewhere have argued that protracted periods in the confines of death row can make inmates suicidal, delusional and insane. Some have referred to the living conditions on death row, the bleak isolation and years of uncertainty as to time of execution, as the "death row phenomenon," and the psychological effects that can result as "death row syndrome." The origins of these concepts are often traced to the 1989 extradition hearings of Jens Soering, a German citizen who was charged with murders in Virginia in 1985 and who fled to the United Kingdom.

Seth texted Junie the next morning to let her know he made an appointment with Raul, the psych guy that she sent over. He knew that would make her happy. Then he added at the end of the message, "let's get together for lunch soon J-girl". He was not sure why he felt possessed to keep typing. He would blame it on the invisible tenants. Lunches weren't really dates after all and Junie Blue was a decent human being. A person could always use decent human beings in their life. Hopefully, he was not harboring ulterior motives or feelings he was not consciously aware of. He seemed to enjoy adding complications to his already tangled existence.

Over the weekend, he took Tillie on a movie date. It seemed a safe public place, and not much talk is exchanged during a show. There was still a slight chill in Till, but she had thawed out for the most part. Seth selected *Guardians of the Galaxy Vol 2* for their viewing pleasure. He loved the first *Guardians* and was looking forward to sharing its odd mix of comedy and action with Tillie.

Witnessing her distraction, he had not selected one that would be her pick of pictures to see. Emma Watson's non-animated version of *Beauty and the Beast* might have been more appropriate. Seth was hovering near the beast category and Till was a beauty… it would be their lives portrayed on the big screen. He was still glad he had chosen *Guardians 2*.

The main character Peter Quill, also known as Star Lord, found out the identity of his formerly unknown father in this sequel. Seth really connected with that theme. However, Peter Quill's dad happened to be a god called 'Ego'. Seth had doubts his dad would turn out to be a god, living on his own planet, which he had in fact created. It was a fun romp from reality, but Tillie did not enjoy the ride.

He invited her to come over for dinner during the week to make up for it. What woman could resist a man who cooked? Hopefully he would be totally forgiven. But as Seth stirred the sauce for his dinner, he began to wonder if he really wanted to be back in Tillie's good graces. He knew relationships took work, but this one felt like he was constructing a dang sky-scraper.

Matilda waltzed into his apartment in a blur of yellow chiffon. She always did make an entrance.

"Smells wonderful Seth. It is so sweet of you to cook for me." Then she spied Barney Fife. "What in the world is that matted ball of fur doing in your apartment? Did you get a dog? Don't you think that is a decision a couple should make together?"

"I was going to introduce you to Deputy Barney Fife. It was not a planned offense, just happened, he followed me home." Seth answered apologetically.

"You have already named him! Did you consider the pound? If you insist on keeping him, I will get you the number for Momma's dog groomer for Pickles, her darling peekapoo." Till offered.

Seth could tell when he looked over at Barney, the maligned dog was not impressed with Tillie either. "I gave him a bath, but kinda like the wild, unkempt look. He looks like a real man's man kind of dog." Seth stood up for his newly acquired canine. He continued to wonder if he and Tillie had anything in common.

The meal turned out not too bad. Chicken Parmesan with garlic bread and a tossed green salad were an overload of carbs for Miss Morgan he was sure, and the garlic could be a romance kybosher. Seth didn't think he was sabotaging things on purpose. Their conversation included the regular job change discussion and other inane things he could care less about. Seth's mind began to wander.

Why hadn't Tillie ever noticed anything unusual or supernatural in his apartment? Then it hit him. Even if an aberration was sitting on her lap, Tillie would never notice, unless it messed up her hair or make-up. Good looks could only take a guy so far. Before Seth knew it, out of his mouth came the words:

"You know Tillster, I have been thinking (for a nanosecond), maybe we need a break to determine if this thing between us is really going to happen. We can see, if absence makes the heart grow fonder, as the saying goes, or just more absent. If we cannot live without each other, we will know it is time to take the next step."

Seth didn't enumerate what that next step would be, he really wasn't sure, and he was improvising. He assumed Tillie thought he was speaking of either moving in, or marriage, and he was getting a strong impression that he wanted neither with this woman. His plan was a stall, to figure how to get out gracefully. There was a chance he could surprise even himself and want back in, but doubtful.

Tillie, caught totally off guard, formed her mouth into an ugly "O" shape with lettuce leaves sprouting out of it. Once she had regained her composure, chewed and swallowed, unruffled Tillie was back.

"I must say I am a bit surprised with this turn of events, Seth, but it may be for the best. We can both accomplish what we need to while apart, to make our lives better when we are back together. For example, you could find the perfect job to surprise me and I could look for apartments and wedding venues. This could be fun. How long should we give it? One month should we say?"

Now it was Seth's turn to nearly choke on his chicken parm. Only Tillie could turn a break up attempt into a joint idea, and a good one at that. Pretty impressive recovery, Till did have a skill set.

"Do you think one month is long enough? You gave us a lot to accomplish. Will we need two?"

"I like a challenge, let's compromise at six weeks." Till decisively responded.

The happily-separated couple toasted on it and Tillie was out the door before nine o'clock to begin organizing their lives together, without Seth. It wasn't even one of their worst dates.

The night was still young, but Seth decided to slip into his sweat pants and watch some TV with Barney. The dog deserved some reward time for the inspiration he had provided in the break up.

Just as they got comfortable, someone knocked. He knew it was too good to be true, Tillie had returned to hash it out.

Seth yanked the door open, but a woman standing on the other side was the polar opposite of Tillie Morgan. Not tall, but not short either, medium build, with medium-length dark curls framing a cheerful face and big brown eyes looking right at him. She was wearing slim cut jeans and a black T-shirt with black canvas converse shoes that had white rubber soles. The girl, closer to a woman, was fresh and youthful in appearance, but not a girl scout, definitely age appropriate for him, maybe in her mid to late twenties.

Before he could even ask, she put out her hand and said, "Hello, I am Halle Valentine with Raul's Psychic Readers, my dad said you were having some paranormal concerns and I am here to help. Didn't we have an appointment at nine o'clock?"

She must have read the surprised look on Seth's face. He had totally forgotten. Normal Seth would have told Halle that and sent her away to come back another day. But new and improved, bolder, grab-the-moment-by-the-balls Seth, wanted this refreshing woman to come in. It seemed Deputy Fife did too. He had joined them at the door and was licking Miss Valentine's hand. Seth assumed she was a Miss…he wanted her to be one.

"Oh yes, forgive me, do come in." Then Seth added awkwardly, "I haven't cleaned up dinner yet, would you like any leftovers before you start?" Where in the world did that come from?

The new girl, not mentioning the obvious, that the candlelit table was set for a romantic dinner for two, responded. "I wondered what that tantalizing smell was and I am starving, sure, if you don't mind. I'll fill a plate and you can fill me in on the situation while I eat."

And before Seth had time to think things through, Halle Valentine, a total stranger, who dealt with even stranger things, was sitting at his cafe-style table eating slightly cold chicken parmesan and garlic bread. If she was that good at directing non-bodied people, she would be a wonder.

"This sure hits the spot. Thanks. Now tell me what you are dealing with and how I can help?"

"Well, I am not really sure what I am dealing with, that is the main problem. And I am not even sure if I am comfortable with your help. Are you involved in the occult or anything of voodoo-ish nature? What is it you do really?" Seth asked.

"How about I just give you a consultation tonight and explain what I do. Then you will be educated to decide if you are interested in my services, before I do anything you are not totally comfortable with." Halle smiled, "How does that sound? No charge, you have already fed me."

Halle was making this easier than Seth thought it would be. "That works for me."

"First, know even though we like to work at night, it is not because we are doing works of darkness. It is just easier to read auras if there is no natural light around. For generations certain members of my family have inherited a spiritual gift, some might call a sixth sense, making it easier for us to tap into things others cannot. Even though it might not look like it, there is an energy all around us, a world wide web that we just can't see. A good psychic has the ability to take a step into a place and pick up on those connections. They can 'tune in' and tap into fantastic insight from issues or themes that seem to be playing out. Einstein talked about there being no real division between past, present and future which becomes very clear when you connect with this web.

My father and I are considered mediums and psychic readers, but he left 'Medium' off our card because it has bad connotations to some people. We do not do séances. A psychic tunes into the aura or energy field of the person they are reading to gather information, while a medium in addition is able to tune into the energy field of a person no longer in the physical body. They are actually able to connect with both spirits who have crossed over and spirits still earthbound, those typically called ghosts. Let me simplify this. There is no scientific evidence of how a mother of an infant knows when her crying baby needs to be fed or to sleep or be played with, she just senses it. Similarly, if you believe in the unknown creator of universe, then you must feel his presence before believing in his creation."

"You believe in God? This surprised Seth for some reason.

"Of course. God is the greatest source of energy and light. His inspiration is a must for me. Not all in my field would agree. There are a lot of well-meaning people doing readings who believe they are psychic and they are not. Then there are some who are psychic, but access other sources that I choose to avoid."

"That makes me feel better for some reason. Let's stay in the light. I work in a dark enough place."

"If we work together Seth, I promise to avoid any dark alleys. I never feel afraid of my dealings with the spirit realm and neither should you. Communication with spirits has one purpose and one purpose only, healing…for the person in the spirit-world and also for the person still in the physical."

"How exactly does it work? You know the communicating part."

Psychics may be clairaudient, or have the ability to hear things; clairsentient, which means they can feel things; or clairvoyant, which simply means that they can see things that most other people can't.

Empaths can tune into the feelings of other people in a very profound way. I have each of these to some degree, but clairsentience is my strongest psychic sense.

The contentment pouring from your dog is currently overpowering the whole room for me. He is one happy boy." Barney's tail began to thud on the floor in agreement.

Every spirit communicates with me very differently. Some will choose to show me a lot of visual images and symbolism, while others prefer to speak to me with thoughts or feelings. As different as personalities are in life, they are in spirit as well. Some spirits are very good at communication through this process and some are just learning, it is as new to them as it may be to you. The most important part of any medium reading is passing on messages from the person in spirit to their family or friends who are still living. Messages can be anything at all."

Seth's skepticism had a chunk whacked out of it. Halle did not seem like most of the wacko's Junie sent. Though her dress and body language communicated youthful and fun, she was also quite knowledgeable in her field and seemed reasonable for a psychic person. He could sense she enjoyed her work and found energy from it. Maybe he was developing some psychic reading tendencies of his own.

"I think I am willing to give this a try." Seth decided out loud.

"What are we trying, Seth?"

"There are unusual events that take place in my place. Things that don't happen, happen. Not only have I seen things, some of my friends and even my dog, have informed me I am not living alone. They don't bother me really. I'm just not sure why they are here, what do they want? Should I be concerned? I just need clarification from a clairvoyant or clairsentient I guess."

"I can tell you without even officially beginning, you do have spirits from the other side here, Seth.

Their presence is strong. There is definitely something they would like to communicate. I would be honored to come back and try to unlock their message for you, if you would like."

"I would like." And I do like, he thought. He did like Halle. She was…what this he was feeling…comfortable. Maybe not a compliment to most women, but it definitely was to Seth. A low maintenance woman sounded incredible. "Let's get me on your schedule."

Just what Seth needed, another person taking up residence in his already crowded head. He could not get Joshua out, now Halle would be residing there for sure, and other spirits popping in and out. It would be wonderful if this woman not only read minds, but decluttered them.

CHAPTER 10

19 states and DC have abolished the death penalty. Alaska, Connecticut, District of Columbia, Hawaii, Illinois, Iowa, Maine, Maryland, Massachusetts, Michigan, Minnesota, Nebraska, New Jersey, New Mexico, New York, North Dakota, Rhode Island, Vermont, West Virginia, Wisconsin.

The day before on Sunday morning, Seth surprised Marion at her Friends of Christ Church for Mother's Day. He slid in next to her on the pew and pinned a carnation corsage on her already flowered dress. Daisies were her favorite flower, but the florist said they would not hold up well, so Seth had settled. Joy spilled from her surprised face as Marion took his hand in hers. It was so simple to share a little piece of himself on the day set aside to honor mothers and that sliver of self, had been the best gift he could have given.

The minister's sermon had been on *Mothers in the Scriptures* and *Is there a Mother in Heaven*? It was interesting to consider that everyone on earth had a mother, even those in cells at Huntsville. He may not have always been the best son, but at least he wasn't incarcerated. Seth was setting a pretty low bar for himself, he could do better. Just spending a few hours to worship with his matriarchal figure and sharing a quick brunch meant so much to her. The older Seth got, the more he realized his mom had made huge sacrifices for him his whole life. It was about time he gave back a smidgen.

Seth remembered growing up he had begged repeatedly for a sibling, preferably a brother. Finally when he was in the seventh grade, Marion doing the best she could with no partner in her life to make his brother-dream happen, signed up to host a foreign exchange student from Japan. The older boy would be attending at Lincoln Prairie High School, where his mother taught, for a school year.

Seth was deliriously excited to have a big brother, Shigeki, for a whole nine months. But before Shigeki arrived, the student exchange committee decided it would be more appropriate to send a girl, Kyoko, to live with a single mother. It did not matter that Marion taught at the school, the decision had been made. A girl was not exactly what Seth had in mind. He did not need a second mother. Having another male figure around the house would have been nice.

Looking back, Seth supposed he did learn some useful skills from Kyoko's stay…he could eat with chopsticks when he ordered Chinese food. But more importantly, he learned how to share his space and accept other people and their cultures. Marion made an effort to make things special for him, even if things did not always turn out exactly how she planned. He truly was grateful for the home she had created for them…

Seth reigned his thoughts back in to his radio show where a caller had just expressed that she was dubious Testerman's wife had absolutely no idea he was doing anything illegal.

Harold Testerman was a brilliant research scientist, who had been fired from the chemical company where he was employed when he ignored all safety guidelines and continued to concoct after-hour formulas he was convinced would save the world. Instead, he blew up half a block of a low end neighborhood near his home and became an official mass murderer.

Harold may have slipped over the line of complete sanity, it was hard to tell, but he was proven competent to stand trial. Seth was not so sure. In testing his theories, Harold caused the deaths of ten innocent people and a feline…a multi-generational family of seven, a young married couple just getting started, plus an old woman and her cat. Harold felt they were collateral damage, necessary for progress in scientific study. It was unfortunate, but if he had to do it over, he probably would do the same thing again. Somehow the loner chemist married, but his mousey wife apparently had absolutely no clue what he was doing outside his regular employment. Or even that he was no longer employed.

"Some husbands can have affairs that their wives know nothing about for years, why do you think hiding another sort of secret life would be any different?" Seth prodded the caller.

"It just seems that if a person were basically a mad scientist, brewing the end of the world in a basement lab, some of the side effects of the work would be brought home with him." she insisted.

"Perhaps his wife did not want to know, and we are not dealing with a communicative man here, but you could be right. Thanks for the call. Who do we have next?"

"Maggie from Milwaukee here. I think Mr. Testerman should be put in an asylum for the criminally insane and allowed to continue his work, or put his genius mind to good use on other projects for the world, not snuff all that intelligence out. Control it, for the greater good."

"Interesting perspective Maggie. I have a caller with an opposing view on the other line."

"Harold Testerman needs to be burned alive; death in the same manner as his victims, who died at the hands of this so called genius, including my daughter and her husband. Maggie from Milwaukee might feel differently if one of her family members were the casualty of this maniac's experimental mind."

Seth let the ladies duke it out for a few minutes on air, never getting too out of hand, before ending both calls with appreciation for their input. Cerebral criminal

Harold Testerman was riling up the audience today. There was time for just one more caller.

"I am calling to recommend you never do a program of this sort, or any sort, about the juvenile convict they are keeping down there in Texas. There are things about him that should never be discussed casually in the light of day. His parentage is not even confirmed. Who knows if we are dealing with mere mortals? Leave this one alone!" The line went dead, leaving nothing but dial tone blaring in the national listener's ears.

"Never a dull moment on Seth Row my friends," Seth stepped in quickly to fill the space, "be sure to tune in next week, but in the meantime, as always America, it has been a pleasure…Seth signing off from the Row, reminding you to *live well and make every day count!"*

Then turning quickly to the team, "What in the world is going on here! Bear, can't we screen these callers a little better. I'm getting battle scars from being blind-sided."

"Sorry Seth, I was manning the phones today, since we aren't on camera." Joey confessed. "That last guy gave no indication he was pulling a mysterious redirect, promise. I would have cut him off at the knees if I'd any idea."

Bear interjected not to fret, crazy callers gave ratings a boost. People loved that kind of drama. Jake was off for the morning, but Gun said he almost cut the sound, but felt it was a powerful way to end the show, a true cliff hanger. Their listeners would be back for more next

Monday. The guys pulled Seth back off the ledge and he calmed down.

"I know you are not much of a drinker Hoff, but let's go get some brews or at least a Coke when we finish up here. There are a few more things I need to run by you, after you defuse." Bear requested.

"Sure man. Sorry guys. Things have just been more insane than usual lately. Let's put another show in the can and call it a day. Thanks amigos."

The crew finished up and headed out. Seth jumped in his CRV and followed Bear to the first pub they passed on the drive home. They entered, far too early in the day, and grabbed a booth together.

Bear nursing a Budweiser and Seth sipping his Coke, started their conversation with a catch up on personal lives. Bear was preparing to 'pop the question' to Ainsley in the next few months and asked Seth for advice on the perfect proposal. Seth was the master at production and Bear wanted it to be memorable. Seth offered to do it on the show, but Bear wasn't sure a show featuring criminals and death, cried out romance.

Then Seth admitted that he and Tillie were on a break, to see if they missed being together. Well, Seth was on the break and Tillie on a planning spree. The two men were like brothers and could communicate much without even speaking, but as afternoon turned into evening they talked. Bear wanted to know about his second momma, Miss Marion. Then as they finally finished running through all the relatives, Bear switched the topic to the recent work situation.

"I have been researching our, quickly-becoming-most-notorious-con, Joshua, as per request and have uncovered some info I think you will find extremely interesting."

"That his parents are not mere mortals, but possible aliens, or better yet, gods who have created their own planets like Ego on *Guardians*?" Seth, in a much lighter mood, jested.

"Not exactly that earth, or universe shattering, but pretty big none the less. Do you know how Joshua ended up at our back door here in Huntsville?

"No, just assumed by assignment."

"Remember reading about the priest, Father Brogan?"

"Yah, that name is a bit deja vu-ish for me."

"Well, according to what I can find, it was the boy's priest, Father Brogan, who made the request to the judge after sentencing. He called in a heavenly favor to place him here."

"Why would that be, Bear?"

"No idea yet, but it gets even weirder. I think, upon further follow-up with phone records, that Father B. from St. Edwards Parish, may also have been the anonymous caller on your show who first notified us of Joshua's pending arrival."

"But why? Why in the world?" Seth wondered aloud.

"That is the golden question, if you figure that one out my friend, we may have an Emmy winning interview with Joshua boy and his posse."

"Looks like I'm a goin' on a road trip to Idaho, Brother Bear. Like to join me?"

"I suggest taking a plane, unless you want to miss a full week of work. Although Idaho sounds tempting, I think I will stay and keep the home fires burning. We have a hot one here." With that last comment, Bear put his finger to his tongue and made a sizzling sound as he pointed towards his business partner, visually punctuating his point.

CHAPTER 11

Bureau of Justice Statistics on Capital
Punishment Lethal Injection Consists of:
Single drug of Pentobarbital

Average Time on Death Row prior to
Execution: 10.87 years

Shortest Time on Death Row Prior to
Execution: 252 days

Longest time on Death Row prior to
Execution: 11,575 days (31 years)

Average Age of Executed Offenders: 39

Oldest Age at time of Execution: 67

Outside the window of the plane, fields formed a
patchwork blanketing the Magic Valley. After years of
erosion, the Snake River cut a deep ribbon, winding
through the fertile valley. Acting as their tour guide, the
pilot shared that two different geographic falls occurred
along this stretch of the Snake.

Twin Falls, for which the city was named, now had one
side of the falls dammed for electricity production. Two
miles west, closer to the city, was Shoshone Falls, which

was actually higher than Niagara with an amazing amount of water flowing over it each spring before the farmers began tapping into the flow to water their crops. Evil Knievel made a failed attempt to jump across the canyon's span on a motorcycle/rocket in the 1970's. If this wasn't an overnight business trip, Seth would have enjoyed some site seeing. Maybe another time when he had someone to accompany him.

Tillie was more than willing to escort Seth on the quick trip, had he encouraged her. She was having trouble defining what 'taking a break' meant. Till even volunteered to tend Barney Fife, but Barney was having a sleepover with Grandma Marion. Seth had finally provided a furry grandchild at least.

If things weren't how they were, Seth might have enjoyed bringing Halle along. She seemed like she would be a more trouble-free traveler than Tillie. He called before he left to postpone her visit to read his haunted rooms for another week. So he was flying solo for a few days.

Seth usually avoided purchasing airline tickets last minute, but found a screaming deal from Dallas to Salt Lake City leaving on Tuesday and returning on Wednesday. Flights to Boise were more expensive, though it would get him an hour closer. He considered renting a car and driving the last three hours, but decided to splurge and booked an additional short hopper flight from a local airline. It would be worth the extra six hours in Twin Falls, he hoped. He hadn't traveled for research in some time.

The airport was tiny, just a landing strip and small building, but Seth was able to rent a car. Public transportation in a city this size would be sketchy. He had reserved a room at the Best Western on Blue Lakes Boulevard, but stopped by the city park on his way to the hotel since it wasn't time to check in yet.

Twin Falls City Park was surrounded on all four sides by roads forming a square. It must have been the city center at one point. Across the street from each side of the park was a public building of minor to major importance. On the far side of the road to the north, was the large ornate St. Edwards Catholic Cathedral with its school next door. The western direction harbored the County Jail and on the south and east respectively were a mortuary and the Twin Falls Public Library. A homeless person in this park had it made, reading, religion, justice and death all covered in one stop shopping.

Green grass and mature trees of both deciduous and evergreen varieties filled the square nicely. A playground was off to the east across from the library and an old stone amphitheater stood near the center. Just behind the amphitheater, Joshua was discovered cradling Jonny's lifeless body.

Seth wandered across the north-side street and up the tall stone steps into the Catholic Church. It was open, as chapels often are, for patrons to come inside to worship. The stained glass windows depicting scenes from Christ's life framed the space and filled it with multicolored rays of light. Seth could use more inspiration in his life. He scanned the room quickly to see if he might be lucky enough to run into the priest, but silence reverberated off the walls echoing in the empty room.

Next door at the school he had better luck. An Officer Truman was just exiting the building and introduced himself as the local law enforcement link responsible for overseeing child welfare issues in the community. He pointed Seth in the direction of the St. Edward's ecclesiastic and educational administrative offices.

There Seth found Mother Mary Catherine who was the headmistress of St. Edward's religious and secular education. She along with two other nuns, Sister Margarethe Helene and Sister Angeline Teresa, represented the church's scholastic needs for the students who attended there.

The size of the school had shrunk in the last few decades, along with the number of woman who chose to take upon themselves the sacred vows. Most of the world did not feel the need for religion anymore, Mother Mary Catherine feared, and their school was down to one small class for each grade at the present time. They hired a few non-nun teachers who were devout Catholics to help cover the diminishing load.

"Are you Catholic young man, perhaps looking for a school for a family member? What brings you to our doors?" Habited and hopeful Mother Mary Catherine asked.

"Actually, I am a believer, but not Catholic, sorry. I am here on other business. Could you tell me anything about the event that took place here a little over a year ago, closer to two years now, in the park, the one involving two of your live-in students?"

Mother Mary Catherine's countenance fell. She was well aware of the tragedy that had taken place. Of course a supposed murderer in their midst did not help the school's population numbers either.

"I hoped that story was old news by now, Mr.… who are you? This is an excellent school. The state has already closed our home for homeless children, and distributed all of them to foster homes. Except Eliza Marie, who has chosen to become a postulate here, she was allowed to remain. Have we not suffered enough?"

"Sister, I apologize, my name is Seth Hoffer. I'm truly not here to cause you more pain, just looking for information. Is there anything you can share with me about Joshua? And perhaps could I speak with Father Brogan before I head back home tomorrow?"

"Mr. Hoffer, everything about that poor young man has been broadcasted to the world I am afraid. He left our establishment a few weeks before the evil took place, I am not sure why. He was always a good boy, a quiet boy, never caused a moments problem when here. He studied hard and was kind to the other children. What happened did not seem in his character. I told the courts that.

Father Brogan is away on church business today, but should be here in the morning. You are welcome to stop back around ten o'clock. We are a small cloister just trying to serve our Lord and his children in this area."

Seth thanked Mother Mary Catherine for her time and her service to her God, then left, promising to return in the morning. On the way out he saw a young woman in a simplified version of nun's garb who must be Eliza Marie, the nun-to-be. Calling her by name, she turned briefly before putting her head down and hurrying by. The girl was as skittish as a church mouse. Either she was not allowed to talk to men at this point of her training or she had been shell-shocked by the school's history. There appeared to be ghosts haunting St. Edwards as well.

After ingesting tasty meatloaf at a local diner, Seth drove around the town before returning to the Best Western and flipping through channels until he fell into a restless asleep. Morning arrived far too fast. He packed, dressed and headed back to the tainted parish wishing he had driven by the falls first, maybe they would have washed away some of the lack of clarity he was experiencing.

Father Sam Brogan was waiting for him in the chapel. The moment Seth entered the sanctuary space, he knew this man standing before him was indeed his father; and not in any Catholic Father sort of way, the long lost Sam. Seth's memories from two years old did not include a clear picture of his father's face, but with every fiber of his being, he just knew. Even the priestly robes could not hide that fact that this man had sired him.

For some unbeknownst reason, Seth also decided at that same moment, he would not give this man who had left him nearly three decades ago, the satisfaction of knowing he knew. Seth could have just placed a phone call to Idaho, but he needed to come in person to behold this Brogan, to look in his eyes and see for himself what he wondered.

"Welcome my son, I heard you were looking for me? How can I be of assistance?"

The 'my son' comment startled Seth for a moment before he realized that was a common salutation for a priest to use… or was there a double meaning there as well? Did his dad know who he was? Was he just messing with him? He wouldn't put anything past Sam Brogan, even if a priest.

"Father, (how ironic), I would like to take a few moments of your time if that is possible?"

"Anything is possible. Take a seat here on this pew and unload not only your feet, but whatever is on your mind."

"I am here to ask you a few things about a young man who used to attend your school, named Joshua. Deep within the court documents, it mentions that you requested to have him sent to Huntsville after sentencing. Could you enlighten me on any reason you would do that?"

The Father looked down at his hands as he answered. "It was because of you Mr. Hoffer, or Seth if I may call you that. I am familiar with your work. I know you to be a fair-minded man, showing compassion to even the condemned. I do not believe Joshua is guilty. I failed him here at St. Edwards and I hoped to perhaps give him a second chance with someone else who might care. I believed you would feel an extra connection to him. Joshua is an amazing young man."

"I don't know if I should be flattered or filled with trepidation. From only brief interactions with him, I would have to agree that there is something unique about the young man. Why do you think he is innocent when a court of law found him guilty so swiftly?

"There is nothing violent or vindictive in that boy. He is a scholar and philosopher, not a fighter. It is not in his character. I have no proof and the prosecution did not seem to be looking for other options, so found none either, but let's just say I have a higher source that tells me otherwise."

"Did you call Seth Row Radio and ask about him?"

"I am afraid I did. I was not sure how else to get him on your radar in a timely manner."

"Did you call again just recently, making strange statements about his possible parentage?"

It was Father Brogan's turn to appear startled. "That one was not from me, I can assure you. I was not even aware a call of that nature took place."

"Is there anything else you can tell me about Joshua that might help as I cross paths and interview him? You realize I have nothing to do with the legal system, I can only bring forth information and shed light on the convict's situation?"

"I do know that, but I had nowhere else to turn. The justice system was not just. No mercy was shown. I have known this young man since he was an infant. He has studied at my knee and lived for the most part in a protected world here at the convent and school. Unless he has hidden tendencies for psychosis, he could not have done the crime he was convicted of. I knew Jonny as well. The boys loved each other as brothers. I believe that is the reason Joshua returned.

He must have known Jonny was in jeopardy. I am not sure what caused Joshua to leave in the first place, perhaps it is all entwined. I do not have all the facts, but hopefully they will unfold before it is too late. Joshua has his own style of communicating, especially since the arrest. He has professed his innocence, but will not fight for himself. I am just asking that you do what you can for one of my sons."

Had the priest exposed a Freudian flash of his hand with his last statement? Did he know who Seth was? The man of God, or at least one who professed to be working for him, should be a poker player for sure. Seth could not read what was going on behind what appeared to be a sincere request for support. Two could play at this game.

"I do my best to be objective and encouraging with every person I interview. I could not live with myself if I did otherwise. These men have nothing left when I cross their paths. I would never abandon them in their time of need." Zinger to the Father, or father, who did abandon a little boy in his time of need. "I will commit to give Joshua due justice and look beyond the obvious, not for you, but for him. Every boy deserves to have a man they can count on in their life."

The conversation was over. They shook hands good-bye. Seth thanked the priest for his time and said he would be in contact at some future junction. Long after Seth left, Father Brogan sat on the pew, his head in his hands, hot tears flowing through his fingers.

 Shame had held him from revealing to Seth who he really was. He wondered if his first born son had any idea. In front of the priest stood a powerful, life-size statue of another famous first born son who had also been betrayed. Rain began to pelt and drain down the stained glass windows. Perhaps heaven was crying too.

CHAPTER 12

Despite numerous security and surveillance measures, escapes from death row do happen. One of the most audacious escapes is that of Charles Victor Thompson, who landed himself on death row in 1998 for the murder of his girlfriend and another man. How did the convicted killer escape? Not by tunneling, he simply walked out the door. All Thompson had to do was smuggle in a suit and arrange a meeting with his lawyer. After the meeting, Thompson switched into his threads and walked out. When he got to the front desk, he was halted by a guard. But Thompson had prepared for this eventuality: He flashed his inmate badge at the guard, telling him he worked for the attorney general. It worked like a charm. Unfortunately for him, Thompson was apprehended three days later after getting hammered at a liquor store in East Texas.

It was already Thursday again. Seth was back in the saddle after being bucked off for a few days by his quick trip to Idaho. His thoughts were left lying back on Twin Falls' fertile ground, focused on another prisoner.

However, Harold Testerman was the star of today's internet show and Seth needed to give Harold his full due, his execution was scheduled for next week. Harold had been ranting about conspiracy theories and spewing numbers. He appeared semi-psychotic. Seth wondered how the system could kill a crazy man, but kept reminding himself this looney scientist killed ten innocent people.

"Mr. Testerman, if I understand correctly, you feel the government has targeted you personally because they are afraid of the work you are doing?"

"You are so naive Seth, they are not afraid, but they want to keep all of us afraid. I do not deserve death, but I prefer it to being incarcerated by a government who will attempt to delve into my mind and purge data from, or place information they select, into my brain."

"I was told that you did refuse a partial-pardon to commute your sentence to life in prison and also requested not to have the lethal injection?"

"Who knows what would really be in that needle, Seth. If their goal is to control us and our minds, I prefer to be executed in a way that they will not have an opportunity. I requested the electric chair or a simple hanging, nothing invasive, methods Texas has used in the past. Hanging was the norm for almost all executions until 1924. The laws changed then and the electric chair became death row's most popular choice. In fact on February 8, 1924, five executions were done in a single day using the chair. Texas has performed multiple executions in a single day on several occasions, in case anyone wants to join my going away party. There is no law prohibiting it, though it has not been done since 1951. If I am hung or electrocuted they will have less opportunity to tamper with my death or any part of me."

Seth was really not sure who 'they' were and he was not sure Harold did either. His goal was not to embarrass the man on his show or take away his dignity before the end. He would not be surprised if the governor ordered a stay of execution to re-evaluate Harold Testerman's sanity after watching this show, if the governor or any of his staff actually opened the online broadcast.

Right now, Seth needed to respond to Harold's last comments before the pause was uncomfortably long, but just long enough for the convicted guest's words to have impact.

"Mr. Testerman, you always arrive so prepared with facts. Thank you for sharing your insights with America. Your mind is a continuous fountain of information and knowledge, who knows what you might have contributed under different circumstances. It will be a loss to the scientific community when you go and is unfortunate that you could not work within the constraints of this world, perhaps you can continue to offer your gifts in the next."

Seth was not sure why he added that last part about Harold contributing in another realm. Maybe because the other world was overlapping this one frequently in his life and he hated to leave the listeners in a negative place. It was getting harder to be edgy, newsworthy and uplifting, which was always his goal. 'Look for the good in the bad', was becoming his new mantra.

Seth signed off with his normal tag line and almost felt like he needed to give Harold a hug before they led him away, but close physical contact was restricted with prisoners. What was happening to him?

The guys invited him to join them for a completion-of-the-show celebratory dinner, where he could fill them in on the findings from his recent trip before the rebroadcast. But Seth bagged off, saying he needed to spend some time with Barney. Even to a dog lover it sounded like a lame excuse.

Seth just had a lot on his mind to process and while the guys were great at brainstorming, he was in more of an introspective mood. He was not ready to share, even with Bear, that he thought he had found his father. Who had become an actual Father. The man went to the ultimate extreme in an attempt to redeem himself in the role.

"Rain check my men. Party hardy for me too. Thanks for pulling off another great show."

Was it great? It was difficult to be objective about what they were doing these days.

Seth entered his apartment to be welcomed by his tail-wagging, tongue-licking roommate. This kind of enthusiasm for his presence was rare, he was glad to be home. Seth decided to order in Chinese for him and Barn. Whomever else was hanging out in his home could get a whiff of timeless oriental spices, a win/win all the way around. Seth placed the call for food, but did not feel settled at all.

Barney Fife reflected his restless mood. The dog paced back and forth, sniffing corners of the room.

Suddenly Seth no longer wanted to be alone or without company that possessed living human anatomy. He wondered if Halle made last minute emergency house calls and dialed her number as well.

The girl and the food arrived together. Seth invited Halle in and paid the delivery boy. Feeling generous, he added a large tip. The boy whooped as he exited down the hallway.

"You elicit strong emotions in those around you it appears, Mr. Hoffer." Halle observed smiling.

"Does your emergency have anything to do with a Chinese dinner?"

"Not really, I had a tough show, the dog was sniffing corners and I did not want to be alone." Seth fumbled. "I hoped maybe you could do part of my reading tonight or at least hang out and give me your impressions. Are emergencies extra?"

"No, once a client, all visits are included at the same price with the package you purchase. It seems I may need to deduct the cost of feeding me every time I come over though. That would be only fair. Hopefully the pungent, yet delicious, smells won't obstruct or detract from any impressions."

Seth looked at the bag of food still in his hands. "Of course, let's eat first. I always think and work better on a full stomach. Then you can purge my demons."

The two comfortably sat down again at Seth's table to share the spicy meal, tossing tidbits to Barney Fife who received them eagerly…hopefully not with a bellyache later. Words came easily as they got to know each other better. Seth shared how he got into Seth Row broadcasting and even a little about Bear and Marion, his closest compadres. They were the important people in his world, but he rarely opened up about his personal life with a business acquaintance. Seth conveniently left Tillie out of the conversation, her presence did not come to his mind.

Halle, which happened to be short for Hallelujah, shared how she had been raised mainly by her father, Raul, and what it was like growing up in a psychic home. She could never get away with anything. Halle had not wanted to follow in her father's footsteps, she went away to college to study her passions, literature and philosophy. But her psychic skills became more pronounced and undeniable.

By her senior year, other students were coming to her on a regular basis for assistance with their paranormal issues and supernatural needs. She did not choose the business. It chose her. She gave up, graduated, and became her father's junior partner. She was now twenty-seven and had been working for him for almost five years. Literature and philosophy still came in handy. The knowledge she amassed at the university helped her decipher some spirits she came across.

Their appetites satiated, Halle got down to business, "I want to read you first and then I will tell you any other presences I detect in the room. After that, you can decide if there is anything you would like me to pursue further, maybe on a follow-up visit. How does that sound?"

"Not so sure I like the idea of being read personally."

"Don't worry, it's not painful or scary, big guy. I will just tell you what I see in the aura that surrounds you or the energy you are presently emitting from your inner self."

"I guess, but stop if I ask you to, okay." Seth requested.

"Your aura is currently low, Seth, like you've been feeling some stress, or something is sapping your energy. Relax, shut your eyes and take a deep breath." The room was quiet for a moment, there was a stillness. "I see three colors surrounding you. An aura is often expressed in the colors of the rainbow, each identify different things that are a part of you. Right now green

133

and orange are radiating around your core or body. Orange reflects a productive nature in your personality that you have a high level of ability for creative expression, are an adventurer, courageous and business focused. Green usually means you are social in nature, content, in harmony, a teacher, communicative, quick-minded, love people and animals." Halle shared.

"Ha-ha, I like what I am hearing so far. What is the other color?"

"Floating around your head is a stronger aura of white, which may be why spirits feel comfortable in your presence and try to connect with you."

What does white mean? I am not saying I believe in all this, but it is interesting research." Seth admitted.

"White is generally present in people who have a spiritual, transcendent nature, those who function in higher dimensions with etheric and non-physical qualities. Your translucent roommates may feel you understand them, Seth."

"Crazy stuff. Not that you are crazy, but this whole concept is new and wild to me. Go ahead and let me know what else or who else you find in my apartment if you can."

At Seth's request, Halle continued. "There are at least three distinct and different energies present that I can identify. The first is a very mature spirit. I think they have already crossed to the other side, but have a connection with you Seth. Could be a family member who is watching over you, a guardian angel of sorts. They are hanging in the background, content, more observing. This is very common. Most of the people I do a reading for have a similar spirit near them. It should be comforting."

"The second presence is not as comfortable, not totally at peace, but they seem to feel safe here with you. Perhaps they are not quite ready to cross. There is an element of timidity or fear of what is next, but a respect for you. You are not in danger. There is no darkness or evil in the presence, but I can feel a tumultuous history. No effort is being made to share anything, just boarding for a bit it seems."

"That one is probably Amos." Seth interjected, "He was a death row inmate who found the light before his death. I found his calling-card in my bedroom one day. Never knew we bonded."

"Those on the other side can see things we often cannot. He trusts you." Halle added.

"Anyone else?" Seth was into this now.

"There is one other young or immature presence, most likely new to the other realm. I believe this soul is trying desperately to communicate, but has not developed the skills needed yet. This one needs time. I doubt it will go anywhere until he or she has shared their message."

"Great. How can we learn to understand the message, so it can leave?" Asked a hopeful Seth.

"Patience. None of the energies here are going to cause you any harm, all will move on when ready. I would not recommend trying to force them out, unless there is a real issue. The first presence will come and go. The second, will be gone for good at some point. And the last one, I can come back in a few days, or next week, to see if the message is any clearer if you would like," suggested Halle.

"So, I am just going to be living with invisible roommates that don't pay rent? No wonder some of my friends find my place creepy. Yes, I want you to come back and share with me any message. It might be important. In fact, I don't really want you to go yet tonight. Want to watch a movie with me and Barney Fife? How about Ghostbusters? Not the new chick version, but the classic original? Don't take offense. I am not making fun of what you do, but it seems like an appropriate parody for the night." Seth speaking too much, too fast, gushed out trying to get Halle to stay.

"I'm not a big movie buff, but it could be entertaining, in a 'research-way' as you say. And I won't even charge you for the time." Halle joked.

Seth popped in the DVD and the two sat down on the soft microfiber couch, with Barney jumping in between them. Seth was willing to give up his favorite chair in hopes of getting closer to the girl, but the dang dog beat him to it. He would have a heart to heart with Barn about date etiquette and how to be a better wingman later. Halle was running her hand along Barney's back, scratching his hard to reach places and the dog looked in ecstasy, lucky beast. Seth threw a blanket over the three of them and they settled down to enjoy the over-the-top comedy about paranormal investigators. He hoped Halle would find it funny.

They viewed most of the movie, laughing and chatting, but before the film finished, all three had fallen asleep overlapping and entwined on the sofa. Barney was out for the count before the opening title flashed across the screen. Halle crashed just after the Ghostbusters creamed the Marshmallow Man. Seth stayed awake for a while watching Halle sleep cuddled comfortably with his dog. Her stray arm draped across his stray dog.

Seth's reservations about having a female stay over evaporated as he watched her slow steady breathing. Halle's brunette locks fell across her peaceful countenance and dark lashes stuck to her cheeks. Seth wondered if he should gently brush the hair out of her face, but hesitated, not wanting to be too forward or mess things up by waking her. He didn't dare move.

He had never been so content around a member of the opposite sex and didn't want her to go yet. Watching Halle dream (hopefully about him) was more absorbing than the video. But by the time the credits rolled, Seth had succumbed to the relaxed feeling in the room and joined the human-canine pile.

CHAPTER 13

Random Texas Death Row Facts:

1) Offenders on death row receive a regular diet, and have access to reading, writing, and legal materials. Depending upon their custody level, some death row offenders are allowed to have a radio. (Items allowed in other states include CD players, coffee pots, library and DVD access, and even pet cats.)

2) One of the most notorious offenders to be executed was a member of the "Bonnie and Clyde" gang. He and another man escaped from Death Row, only to be captured and returned. He was executed May 10. 1935.

3) The State of Texas has executed brothers on six occasions.

The trio woke the next morning still tumbled together on the couch. The situation somehow not nearly as awkward as it should have been. Halle's hair was all tousled and her make-up for the most part had vacated her face, but she did not seem to care. She just chuckled about having slept with a man she barely knew, but found comfort in the fact she at least read his aura first.

Seth's no overnighter rule had been unintentionally broken with no regrets. Tillie would be irate.

Halle gathered her few things, a backpack-type purse and phone, and thanked Seth for the nice night…treating her to both dinner and a show, ha-ha. She reminded him to let her know when he would like her to come back to see if she could interpret the invisible newbie's message. Seth promised he would be in-touch as she swooshed out the door sucking some of the room's energy and light with her.

Seth wondered what color her aura was along with everything else about her. He realized he was actually more attracted to her brain or what lay beneath her skin, than her body, though there was nothing wrong with her body either. Maybe it was her essence, the total package that mesmerized him. Halle was a unique girl. She may be the first woman that really fit in his unconventional world. He could almost imagine a future Halle Hoffer….what was he, in junior high?

Seth was still reliving last night, when his mom arrived bearing coffee and donuts.

"Good morning Seth! I thought if I dropped by this early, I might catch you still at home and surprise you with a little non-nutritious breakfast."

"Always a pleasant surprise Ma." Seth lifted an old-fashioned and a Bavarian cream filled donut out of the specialty box. "But I know you, there is always more to the story. What's up?"

"In truth, I was a little worried about you after yesterday's show. You did not sound like yourself, son. I just needed to see for myself if you are okay. Did something happen on your trip? And who was that darling little brunette I just spoke with in the hallway? She seems delightful."

"Both of those questions will take much longer to answer properly than I have time this morning, but I can give you the crib note condensed versions."

"I am willing to take whatever you can give, please put an old mother's mind at rest."

"Neither are very rest-inducing answers I am afraid. I have not told anyone yet, but I think I found dad. It looks like long lost Sam is now a Catholic priest living in Idaho," revealed Seth.

"Certainly you must be mistaken, Seth."

"I don't think so Mom, I am pretty sure it was him, but I am going to check things out further."

"Now that would be a bigger surprise than my donut breakfast! And what about the natural beauty? Do you have a new female figure in your life again? What happened to Tillie?"

"Her name is Halle Valentine, you actually met her father Raul, at my door one night before I got home. Remember?" Marion nodded her head that she did. "Well, she was here to give my apartment a psychic read since so many odd things have happened. Tillie and I are on a break."

"This, Halle, had a very warm smile Seth. I have a good feeling about her, she has something instantly like-able. Try not to let your strange life run her off too."

"Not likely mom, Halle likes my strange life more than I do. She is even making friends with it. Just wait until she reads your aura. And for the record I did not run Tillie off." Yet, he thought.

Marion's concerns abated a bit as she ingested some mother/son time. She was never one to wear out her welcome and was gone before an hour had passed.

Seth showered, shaved, ignored Tillie's phone messages and texted Junie B.: "Just wanted to alleviate your fears and let you know I finally had one of your paranormal people come by. You can stop sending them. You were right my friend, I do have translucent visitors. Luckily they appear, or disappear ha-ha, to be harmless. Thx for having my back. Hope we cross paths soon."

There, that was a save, he moved Junie back to the friend-zone gently. Now she would not be expecting a lunch date anytime soon. Junie really was a great girl. Maybe he should set her up with one of the guys. Gun had a girl, but Joey and Jake were available. What was he thinking, he had enough on his plate without adding matchmaker to his many tasks. 'Seth Row Relationship Specialist', that would be a laugh. His specialty was ending relationships, not starting them, his two decades as a bud-couple with brother Bear probably didn't count.

The bathroom was still steamy as Seth wiped off the mirror to complete his final grooming needs. Over his shoulder he saw what looked like words written on the foggy shower door. Turning around to see more clearly, there was definitely something scrawled on the glass that could not have happened brushing by with a body part or towel.

The marks looked like letters of the alphabet, but did not spell any words Seth was familiar with. He jotted down 'non peccavimus' before the letters evaporated with the rest of the moisture into the air. His metaphysical friends were back.

Seth phoned his friend in the flesh and asked Bear if he could meet him for lunch at Campuzano's. This Friday they did not have a Seth Row Special. Death row was slow for the next few weeks, thank goodness. Seth needed to share his father-findings with his best bud before he heard elsewhere and also felt the need for Mexican food. The combination sounded satisfying.

Over his plate of shrimp fajitas and Bear's chimichanga, Seth shared the story of his encounter with Father Brogan, thee father Brogan. Bear, like Marion, was skeptical at first. But Seth was not known to jump to conclusions. What were the odds that this Joshua case would lead them to Seth's Sam?

"Are you sure Seth? That is mondo huge!"

"Ninety-nine percent sure. I want to verify it, but my gut tells me it is indeed so."

"What do you plan to do with you new-found double father?" Bear asked.

"Not sure yet. Father Brogan doesn't know, I know. I want to think things through first. But I wanted you to know why I have been so distracted since I got back. I also had my apartment sort of supernaturally de-bugged, or at least unmasked. It has been a busy week."

"Hey Seth, why don't you take a few days off the first of the week to figure all this new news out. I can handle things on the Row. 'Bear Row Radio' has a nice ring to it, don't you think? And if I don't feel like I can put off the interviews, I will post-pone the guests and play a 'best-of' re-run. No sweat. How about it? I can even put the team on the scent of the priest and have us all digging on the mysterious Joshua?"

"I'll take you up on the offer. I am only running on half my cylinders lately and my brain is clogged with more than you know." In his mind Seth was listing them …Sam, Joshua, Junie, Tillie, Halle, Amos, the unknown dead family member and young spirit trying to communicate.

"I will owe you Bear-man. I haven't even asked you about Ainsley and the proposal. My bad, sorry to be so absorbed in my own stuff lately."

"All's good man, we can catch up on me next time. I plan to propose to Ains on the Fourth of July. You know, since she is the fireworks in my life, seems appropriate don't you think? She has been talking kids and I need to make it legal before we add any new little Buckley's to the team."

Seth could think of several other analogies to go with that holiday. The day celebrating liberty and the Declaration of Independence did not scream 'I want to be bound to you in wedded bliss forever', to him anyway. He wondered if Ainsley would give up cheerleading to have children, the image of Ainsley on the Cowboy grid-iron dancing with a basketball, or maybe football, shaped belly was both mesmerizing and disturbing at the same time. But Seth only said out loud to his buddy, "Let me help however I can, I'll even be your Cyrano de Bergerac if needed."

"You don't have a big enough nose and would probably steal my girl too, but we'll work out something. Thanks, Seth." Bear went back to the thorough clearing of his plate, the chimi with beans and rice did not look like it would be enough to satisfy his large appetite.

"One more quick question Bear, do you have any idea what the words 'non peccavimus' mean?"

"No idea Seth, but you were always more the scholar than me. They sound like Latin. Just Google them."

Seth didn't know why he had not Googled them before, perhaps subconsciously he did not want to know.

Especially, when he was alone in his haunted bathroom, but now he hastily typed the thirteen letters onto his phone key pad. Upon the screen appeared the words *'Latin for not guilty'*.

The men finished their meal in relative silence, having said what needed to be said. Their bromance was intact and had carried them through tough times before. Both sat reflecting on their futures, as they chewed tortillas.

CHAPTER 14

The first recorded execution in Texas occurred in 1819 with the execution of a white male, George Brown, for piracy. In 1840 a black male, Henry Forbes, was executed for jail-breaking. Prior to Texas statehood in 1846, eight executions, all by hanging, were carried out. Upon statehood, hanging would be the method used for almost all executions until 1924. Hangings were administered by the county where the trial took place. The last hanging in the state was that of Nathan Lee, a man convicted of murder and executed on August 31, 1923. The only other method used at the time was execution by firing squad, which was used for three Confederate deserters during the American Civil War as well as a man convicted of attempted rape in 1863. Texas changed its execution laws in 1923, requiring the executions be carried out on the electric chair and that they take place at the Texas State Penitentiary at Huntsville (also known as Huntsville Unit)

Seth lay wide awake staring up at the ceiling. It was after two o'clock A.M. and eerie light from his laptop screen danced off the walls, ricocheting around the ceiling casting cyberspace shadows. The crown molding looked mottled. He had not used a nightlight since he was ten, but he did not feel safe nor secure in pitch blackness within his walls anymore. Seth had considered getting a gun, but realized the ridiculousness. He placed his old wooden baseball bat under his bed for protection, but again what good would that do? Barney had become a watch dog and slept at the foot of Seth's bed enabling him to relax minimally.

Who had written the cryptic message in the mist? Definitely not Amos, he confessed his guilt. His guardian angel? Not likely, sounded like he was more an observer of the three ring circus. Man-boy could have joined the paranormal party, but again, he professed his guilt. And Harold had been given a one month stay of execution to allow for another set of psychiatric testing, so he was still in his physical form. Seth would certainly have noticed Harold in the shower. That left mystery guest number three. The one Halle had felt was still learning to communicate. His skills seemed to be improving rapidly if so.

Seth slid the laptop off the nightstand onto the bed. He may as well make these after midnight hours productive. Typing 'Priests in Idaho' into the empty search box at the top, several options came onto the screen. He had not known there was a 'Priest Lake, Idaho' in the northern part of the state, but chose to click on the 'Diocese in Boise' instead. Several faces, whom Seth assumed were Catholic clergymen in black dress with white collars, appeared on the page.

At the very top next to a man dressed in red robes was the name, Bishop Peter F. Christensen, (ironically, even Christian was in his last name Seth noticed) with the date May 25, 1985 beside his picture. Brown eyes, short brown hair covered with a red skull cap, cleft chin and slight smile, starred out at him in the dark room. The man did look like he would be able to console a troubled soul. The date must represent when he was ordained or whatever they called it in the Catholic Church when they took their vows.

Under Bishop Christensen were nearly ninety men of various ages and ethnicities with a 'Fr.' before their names. Some were listed as retired. These white-collared men must be the Fathers or Priests around the state of Idaho. Although 'Fr.' could also stand for Friar, if they lived in the days of Robin Hood. Seth had no idea there would be so many. They all looked like they were probably nice men, however there were a few he might worry about confessing his sins to. Who knew from a picture really? Seth scrolled down the pages until he saw the familiar face. There it was official ...

Fr. Sam T. Brogan,

St. Edward the Confessor, Twin Falls,
and Our Lady of Guadalupe, Twin Falls

December 25, 2000

There must be two Catholic Churches in Twin Falls, perhaps was why Father Brogan was out when Seth first went to St. Edwards? And the date, interesting, Sam became a Priest the same year Joshua was born, less than a year after for sure. He wondered what the significance of that could be, perhaps nothing.

Seth opened a few more sites reading information on the infamous case in Idaho before he was drowsy enough to dose off for a few hours before it was light.

Seth was still in the thick lack-of-sleep haze when Bear called the next morning.

"I know you're taking a few days off for R and R, but drop by the office if you can. We uncovered something you are going to want to see. It will be well worth your trip in, Bro."

Seth didn't shower or shave before he dropped by work. In addition to his current small aversion to his bathroom company, he was on vacation. He hadn't been in the Row building for a few days. Bear had done a bang up job as fill-in host and he had not been needed until now. Bear and Jake were hunched over a computer screen when he walked in. Joey, the resident computer whiz, aka hacker, was seated on the chair manning the keyboard. He had somehow unearthed from the deep dungeons of the State of Idaho Vital Records a birth certificate they all wanted Seth to see.

"You may want to take a seat before you read it, Seth. This info is enough to knock you off your feet."

Seth saw he was looking at a birth certificate for Joshua. Josh's mother's name was listed as Eliza Marie with the family name as 'Brogan'. Seth sat stunned, he felt like he had been punched in the gut by a heavy weight boxer, but continued reading. The line for the father's name was not filled in, but Seth had his suspicions. Sam must have traveled the country after leaving him and his mother, making other little boys to abandon, and the fact he was now a priest was disgusting.

"Did you find anything on this mother, Eliza Marie? That name sounds familiar."

"No, but look at the bottom of the record. Joshua's birth was a twin birth. There may be another little Joshua or Joshetta out there somewhere, unless his twin died at birth." Joey pointed out. "This record was in a hidden file, not with the mainstream records. Someone did not want this baby to be found."

"I have a sneaking suspicion who that may be. Anyone willing to take a bet our favorite priest had a hand in it? Catholic Fathers are not really supposed to be creating children, just tending to those our Father in Heaven has already created. I need to make a call to Idaho."

Seth dialed St. Edwards School and spoke with Mother Mary Catherine, who informed him the priest was away for a few days on a personal emergency. Father Brogan could have several emergencies in his life on a regular basis, Seth imagined. She took a message and said she would have him call when he returned. Seth pressed, saying it was of grave importance, but the nun did not know how to reach Sam and apologized. Wouldn't it be nice to be able to disappear as easily as his nefarious father?

Frustrated, Seth thanked Joey and Bear for their stellar efforts and headed home to follow the leads he had available. They promised to call if they found anything else.

Seth supposed he could have stayed at the offices searching with the others, but his mind worked best solo. It was weird, but he felt the spirits in his apartment wanted to help him find the things he was looking for too. He had two teams to work with, on both sides of earth's curtain, he joked to himself. He turned off his phone for more focus and delved in. Seth was not a detective, but his criminology studies and journalism skills gave him an edge in deciphering data.

After a few hours, there was a knock at his door. At first Seth decided to keep working and just ignore it, but the person on the other side was not going away, instead the rapping was getting more insistent. Barney waited expectantly and jumped up on his paws to escort his master to the door when Seth finally gave up and answered the pounding.

This was a day for surprises. Seth immediately figured out what, or at least where, Sam's emergency had taken him. Either Junie B. had called in an exorcist, or the rumpled priest at his threshold was Father Brogan in the flesh.

The man was not as priestly appearing as he had been before. His eyes looked haunted and his face haggard. It was apparent he had not shaven in the past few days and his attire was quite wrinkled. Sam could use a shower and some rest.

Seth wondered how a priest would get along with ghost number three in the family bath. Father Brogan waited to be invited in, while Seth pondered his options. He did want to speak with the priest, but was not sure he really wanted him in his home. Maybe he should invite Marion over and they could have a sad little family reunion.

Finally Sam broke the silence. "I did not tell you everything when you were in Twin Falls, Seth. I have been on a bus for forty-eight hours to get here. Could I please come in for a few moments?"

Seth wanted to say no, and slam the door in this deserting liar's face, but his journalistic curiosity got the best of him. What could this man come up with to say in his own defense? He really would like the whole story.

"You can come in on my conditions. You promise to tell me the truth, the whole truth and nothing but the truth, so help you God. And leave immediately, with no discussion when I ask you to." Seth outlined.

"I can live with that. I am not the monster you must think," the man of the cloth, that needed an ironing, responded.

"Oh, and no defending or making excuses for yourself, just the unemotional facts." Seth interjected.

"The no emotion part may be difficult. It seems you know who I am. I am so sorry, Seth."

"No apologies. Only the facts. I knew who you were the moment I laid eyes on you, you scumbag. I'll try to be professional, but it would almost have been easier to find out you were dead, than alive, strutting around pretending to be a religious man while you continued to be a stud service for other sons."

"Oh my, oh my no…you know even more than I thought. It is not what it seems Seth. Please give me a chance to explain. I know you are sharp, I have followed your career with a father's pride."

"You do not deserve to even say that. I am no longer a Brogan, if you hadn't noticed."

"Oh, I noticed, with deep regret, even though I knew it was fair. I was not there for you Seth, but it is not what you think. I was weak and ashamed. I felt you were better off without me. I have lived my life to try to make amends." Sighed the deflated father.

"Just explain to me one thing, is Joshua also your biological son?"

'That is another story," the priest deferred.

"A simple yes, or no, will do!"

"Yes." Sam admitted.

'You sicken me. I did not think even you could stoop so low, tell me, was his mother a nun? The name Eliza Marie sounds familiar."

"No Seth, she was not a nun at the time and I was not a priest. Eliza was a postulate, studying to take her vows when we fell in love. I worked at the convent and school as a handy man to help however I could. After I left you and your mother, I was lost and not sure what to do with my life. I wandered aimlessly for few years doing odd jobs around the country. I wanted absolution I suppose, and turned back to my Catholic roots settling in a small town in Idaho to live out my days anonymously. I did not mean for it to happen, but it did. Eliza was a lovely gentle woman who, after we met, felt her higher calling was to be a wife and mother. So we were married by Father Fitzgerald, he was the priest at St. Edwards at that time. I continued to work for the parish and so did Eliza. It was a peaceful place and time."

"Get on with it. I am not here to hear your replacement love story." Seth spewed the words from his mouth.

"Eliza became with child, but she was a tiny woman and she was carrying two babies, twins. Her pregnancy was complicated and the babies came early. Eliza did not recover from their birth, but both babies lived. Now, instead of a second chance, I had ruined another family's lives. I hadn't known how to provide for one child, now I had two more, with no mother. I gave them over to the convent to raise at the school and orphanage. My grief was so great, I prayed to die. Father Fitzgerald is the one who suggested I study to be a priest."

"How is that even possible?! I thought priests were supposed to be celibate, not in competition to see who could physically 'father' the most children! And you had been married, twice!"

"That is what I thought too, Seth. But Father Fitzgerald informed me that there are a hundred married priests in the United States alone today. He saved my life. I will never marry again. I have dedicated my life to God. I can be a priest, but never a bishop. I am content where I serve. We decided it was best for the twins to never know I was their real father, but I could look after them as their spiritual father, Father Brogan. I thought it was working out well. Until Joshua went missing, only to return a few weeks later to be accused of Jonny's murder. It has been nightmare."

"Do you realize that this nightmare has you as the central boogieman? And you keep saying twins. Is Joshua's twin still alive?"

"Yes, I think you may have met her briefly. Eliza Marie, the young postulate from the school. She was the only live-in student allowed to remain. I had to fight hard to keep her there."

"So I have a half-sister as well?! The taser shocks just keep coming." Seth sat down in his comfortable chair to compose himself. Barney sat beside him and licked his dangling hand. The dog had an emotional barometer and could sense his master's pain. Seth wanted to ask the priest to leave, but instead out of his mouth came the words, "Do you need a place to stay? You could probably crash on my couch tonight and I can drop you off at the bus in the morning, unless you would like to see Joshua before you go back. I am meeting with him to shoot some clips this week and could move it up to tomorrow."

"That is more than I can ask for my son," reverently replied the priest.

"Please don't call me that, in whatever aspect you are using it, it makes my skin crawl."

"I apologize, it is a habit and I do consider you a son, even if I have done nothing to deserve the relationship, maybe one day…."

"Unless I convert to Catholicism, doubtful. Just enjoy the couch and we can figure the rest out in the morning. The bathroom is down the hall, you look like you could use a good scrubbing." Seth tossed the bedraggled Father a blanket before exiting to the privacy of his bedroom to digest and regurgitate the things he had just ingested.

What would Marion think about his new roomie? Ten to one, she'd find this robed man more haunting than his sheet-less ghosts.

CHAPTER 15

The youngest person ever executed in the U.S.
during the 20th Century was a teenage boy
George Stinney Jr. convicted of murdering two
young girls in 1944. George was black and just
14 when he was sentenced to death over the
killing of two white girls, aged 11 and seven.
He was later exonerated 70 years after he was
sent to the electric chair for the crime. Today
a person has to be at least 16 to be executed
in the U.S.:
SIXTEEN AND ABOVE (1 state) North
Carolina
SEVENTEEN AND ABOVE (5 states) Georgia,
Louisiana, New Hampshire, South Carolina,
Texas
EIGHTEEN AND ABOVE (25 states) Alabama,
Arizona, Arkansas, California, Colorado,
Delaware, Florida, Idaho, Indiana, Kansas,
Kentucky, Mississippi, Missouri, Montana,
Nevada, Ohio, Oklahoma, Oregon,
Pennsylvania, South Dakota, Tennessee,
Utah, Virginia, Washington, Wyoming.

The force field between the two worlds was in flux all
night long. Lights turned on and off sporadically, even

the television turned on once for no apparent reason. Seth was not sure if those-he-could-not-see were excited or rebelling against the priest sleeping on the sofa. Whatever their motivation, they were busy boys.

Seth let Father Sam fend for himself in his kitchen the next morning scrounging up breakfast. He fed Barney and grabbed a granola bar and Coke for himself. Fuel for their Huntsville shooting spree, shots only in the camera-sense of the word.

Bear had been exasperated that Seth allowed the priest on a ride along. Their travel-talk was hampered by the man in black. The rest of the guys found it entertaining and their guest intriguing.

They anticipated Emmy quality interactions from the combination of characters…Father and sons (all of them), father and son (Seth) and father and secret son (Joshua)…the cinematic combos were endless. Seth hoped he hadn't orchestrated the road trip from hell.

It turned out to be surprisingly easy to get a man of God into the prison. Conceivably the team could keep an extra set of robes in the van for prison visit emergencies, if not too sacrilegious.

Warden Walker gruffly greeted them and showed them to the usual area they used for production. He'd heard through the grapevine that the network was looking to broadcast a live execution and considering Huntsville's latest young celebrity. Walker had concerns and was going to "watch them all with hawk eyes using night vision googles". The image was intense, but a comic relief for Seth. Maybe they could make another Birdman movie with the warden. But the other idea, of a live execution, was repugnant. He hoped to never be a part of such a production.

Sam the priest was in his element, visiting with every prisoner whose path he crossed as if campaigning for a future penal transfer. While Seth, Bear, Gun, Jake and Joey wired the room. A couple of the inmates who had received permission to assist as production apprentices, helped with the process. Theoretically, learning a skill they could use on the outside one day.

After about thirty minutes a bound Joshua was led into the room. His impassive face not able to hide surprise at seeing the priest as he entered.

Father Brogan requested a few minutes alone with the boy which Seth denied, saying maybe when they finished. Seth wondered if perhaps the priest wanted to offer the condemned man a final confession or what his motivation might be. For now, Father Brogan needed to make himself invisible, one of his better talents. The Priest was escorted out of the room to watch through soiled glass.

Joshua was less than engaged in the charade. Seth wondered why the boy even allowed himself to be a part of their show when he looked so bedraggled and forlorn about the escapade.

Icy gray-green eyes peered from hollows in Joshua's face. "I have already shared all I know."

"You were never put on the stand. Think of this as a time to speak on behalf of yourself and share anything that might shed some light or understanding the courts may have missed," ventured Seth. "You could tell us about your sister?"

"Never. How did you find out? Please, if you have any mercy in your exposing heart, Eliza must be protected from all this. I will not say a word, until I have your word she will not be identified in any way. It does not matter what happens to me."

"Of course, if that is your wishes. Off the record I would like to know more, but that can wait."

Turning to the production team, "Guys, please make sure any references to Eliza are edited out of the final piece. Okay Joshua, what would you be willing to share?"

The teen's eyes gained light, glowing from their depths in the grayness. "Once there was a small fold of sheep, watched over by a hired shepherd, because their master was far far away. A wolf in sheep's clothing entered into their midst, the caregivers unaware. The wolf looked like the sheep, but under his wooly coat was hidden what he really was. One of the original sheep saw beneath the surface and wandered off looking for safety among greener pastures. He was cast as a black sheep or purple sheep or marked in an identifiable way as less than desirable, when under his wool beat the heart of a real lamb. He tried to find a safer spot for the others, whom he had grown to love as they grazed together, but he was just one lost sheep. Now branded. The mother ewes had left their baby lambs as well. They were so vulnerable. They did not recognize the wolf, until it was too late, and he carried off one of the littlest lambs. The sheep-herder, filling in for the master, was released from his fulltime duties with the rest of the flock. Only one little ewe still roamed the fold fearing for her safety, but not knowing where else to go. So she pulled another cloak around herself and hoped to be hidden and not betrayed."

"Tell us the meaning of your story? Are you the black lamb Joshua?" Seth almost whispered.

"We are all black lambs I fear, or like the little ewe, unable to see the wolves in sheep's clothing around us."

"Why don't you lead us to the wolf? Save those you can?"

"I cannot. I am sorry." Joshua was solemn.

"Are you the wolf?"

"If I were the wolf, I would have devoured myself. No, the beast is not I."

"I want to understand why you will not defend yourself? Help us." Seth pled.

"There are things that cannot be seen and things that cannot be said. Truly, it does not matter what happens to me at this point. I am at peace….as long as Liza is safe…I can leave the disbanded fold in peace."

"What do you know about your parents?" Seth asked.

"Nothing. Only that they did not want me."

"What if I told you that I have seen your birth certificate and know who you mother is, her name was also Eliza. She did want you, but could not keep you. She died shortly after your birth."

"Then I shall see her soon… After I am gone, could you let Eliza know she was not abandoned by everyone in her life, on purpose anyway? That would be the greatest gift you could give me."

"Yes, I promise to speak with Eliza. Anything else? I am struggling to make sense of this. Help me Joshua."

"Help I can no longer give, but it is there all around you, you just must be open to and access it." Joshua paused.

The young man, suddenly drained of whatever shone from his eyes, slumped forward. The extra battery pack of energy that had been propelling him had run out. Seth, feeling compassion, said they could be done for the day. Sam began slapping the window and pointed to his chest.

"Father Brogan would like a few minutes with you Josh, if you are not too worn out."

"I would prefer not to see him, but I suppose it doesn't matter either way."

Before going back to his nine by six foot bleak cell, Joshua's home away from home, the Seth Row team gave the priest and his second biological son a few moments alone to catch up. Seth would have loved to remain in the room and see what went down between the two. He wondered if Sam would let the boy-convict know the other father role he also held in the boy's life, the one he had kept hidden. Was he better to this son than he had been to him? Maybe it was easier to be loving when it was from behind the mask of the priesthood. But if Seth had to pick, he would rather be standing in his own shoes than his half-brother's.

The boy did not look comfortable at all. He was obviously not excited to see his religious leader. Was it due to the feeling he had let the man down or from being let down himself? It was hard to tell. Was the teen inmate an accomplished actor? Had he committed the crime and feigned his innocence? If not, did he know who the actual murderer was? Was he covering for someone and if so why?

Josh did not look frightened, but some dynamic was off. What else had elusive Sam left out of the family equation? Seth still had more detective work to do. After five minutes the male bonding moment between the two was over and with it whatever Seth might have learned from eavesdropping.

The ride back to Waxahachie was not any better than the ride there. Bear sulked, Father Brogan ruminated and Seth felt like his brain was exploding with all the pressure of sorting through input from the past few weeks. He was unusually more objective and aloof with the facts he dealt with daily, but this time it had become considerably too personal. He could not see clearly.

Seth's phone vibrated. As a rule, he did not take calls on this drive. This was time to debrief with Bear about their projects, but the car was quiet and Bear was behind the wheel, so Seth picked up the call. Their producer from the network, Brin Gillette was on the line. Brin was a powerful woman in the TV world, but her normal business persona sounded almost giddy with excitement as she laid out her newest idea and proposal.

She confirmed what warden Walker had alluded too. NBC wanted to be the first of the mainstream channels to broadcast a live execution. Brin felt America was ready for it. Violence in the media sold news. The escalation of videos on YouTube and other internet sites with the highest volume of viewers were from three main categories…porn, music videos and violent acts. She had a vision of a Seth Row Special combined with, or ending with, a live televised execution. The execs felt that the combination of a notorious, yet also sympathetic character, like the young convict currently being held in Huntsville, would be dynamite in their lineup. They were giving Seth the 'ultimate opportunity' to host the execution of his brother. However, she did not add the identity of the teen, Seth nonverbally did.

Sickness filled his soul. Seth listened to the cheery plans of his superior droning on and on. There was absolutely no way he wanted to take any part in this gruesome exploitation, but he could not get the words out. His intent was, always and forever, to bring people to life not slay them on air. Instead of answering, he feigned a poor connection and promised to call Brin back when he was back in the office.

He needed time to review his contract with NBC and see if there was a way around participating in this ugly death-for-dollars scheme. His two car mates remained oblivious to the impending plot of the next Seth Row Special and Seth wanted to keep it that way for the rest of the ride. This kind of carsickness would be catching.

CHAPTER 16

It is rare for a woman to be given the death sentence in the United States. Of the 3,146 persons on death row in the U.S. as of February 2013, only 61 of them, or 1.9 percent, were women. Of the 61 women who were on death row in 2013, 13 of them were convicted of killing their husbands and/or boyfriends, 12 were convicted of killing their children and two killed both their husbands and their children. Only 568 female executions have been documented since 1632, which constitutes 2.8% of the total known executions in the United States since 1608. Since 1973, 162 women have been sentenced to death, and only 11 have been executed. That is less than 1% of the 1,099 executions since 1976. The last female executed was in Texas in 2005. Currently, there are 51 women on death row, which comprises 1.5% of the 3,350 persons.

Seth and Bear dropped Sam off at the bus station as they drove into town. It was time he headed back to his parishioners. Seth knew the right thing to do was to spring for a flight back to Idaho for the priest, but he was still too angry. Mostly out of guilt, he slipped the priest a 'Benjamin' for any extra expenses he may incur on the journey. It felt like shelling out money as the collection plate passed in church. They said brief good-byes with Father Brogan mumbling he would be in touch.

Seth just nodded. Either way he would survive, this man was just another complication in his life. He wasn't feeling the fatherly vibe. Seth chose not to mention the dilemma he faced from his recent phone conversation with Brin Gillette. Maybe a man of the cloth could have given him some insight on the matter, but he was used to winging it without any kind of father.

When the priest had vacated the car, Seth did share with Bear about the call he had received on the drive. Bear, already frustrated from the tag-along, nearly exploded. An exit clause to release them from doing the live execution didn't come to mind, but he said he would go over the contract with a fine tooth comb and bring in their lawyer on it as well. Even though Bear was used to 'killing' the opponent on the football field, killing someone on camera, came too close to terrorist footage in his book. Seth was glad they were in sync on this one. They still had some time to get this figured out.

Seth's coping mechanism to deal with stressful situations was to change track and focus on something else for a few days. He had another sticky wicket happening with his love life which would help distract him. His six week separation from Tillie was coming to its D-day culmination.

So, Seth decided to deal with his lady loves, putting the women in his life in order needed some TLC too. Not over-thinking the Seth Row Special request might give some time for his thoughts on it to drop into place, like on a game of tetras. He never was good at that game.

First on his list was Junie Blue. He had put her off with texts for long enough, so Seth met her for lunch at the Dove's Nest. The quaint restaurant was sort of a chick gathering spot in Waxahachie's historic downtown.

Home-cooked southern food was served up, surrounded by home furnishings and antiques. Seth hoped that Junie would draw a gay-guy-friend-type vibe (even though he was straight) and not think it cried romance.

He need not have worried, Junie was cool. She arrived with her thick auburn hair cut in a current style, chin length with one side buzzed off. Seth usually found the look a bit butch, but Junie pulled it off. She was dressed for fun, not to seduce, with a Dallas Cowboy's jacket over slacks. J.B. had so much going for her. He wished things could have been different between the two of them, but they made much better friends than they did a couple.

Seth thanked her for her concern about the supernatural happenings at his house and told her he was finally using someone she had sent. Junie picked up on the more-to-the-story dialogue and Seth confessed he liked the paranormal reader she sent as more than a psychic. Laughing at providing matchmaker services, Junie admitted she had not planned on sending a blind date for Seth, but was happy he found someone who might be able to understand him and his invisible roommates. She shared that she never thought Tillie was right for him in any way. Then was embarrassed to find out the two were still together, for now, and tried to suck back some of her words. Finally she embraced them.

"You know Seth, you deserve better than Tillie Morgan. I know to the eye she has it all, but you two are not a good match. If it cannot be me in your life, keep looking. Your new little psychic friend may be just what you need. Even if her name, Hallelujah Valentine, sounds like it belongs to a My Little Pony. And you know I will always be there for you, in whatever capacity works for us."

The pressure was off with girl number one. Junie B. graciously remained in the friend-zone at the Dove's Nest. If he was filming an episode of The Bachelor she might not have received a rose, but might be voted Miss Congeniality by the rest of the cast. Too bad things probably would not go as smoothly with girl number two…aka Miss Matilda Morgan.

Tending to Tillie took much more finesse. Meeting in a public place was essential for two reasons.

172

One, a home cooked meal at his place would not be reward enough in her eyes for their time apart, unless Seth planned to offer dessert in the bedroom following dinner. And two, they needed to be in a location that prevented her from expressing the full extent of her wrath if things went sideways.

Seth arrived early at Five Sixty by Wolfgang Puck on Reunion Blvd…appropriate street name if she noticed the detail…to set the stage and create a positive opening. Other patrons recognized him, most just stared, but a few brave souls spoke.

Until Tillie made her normal, or even above normal if possible, impactful entrance. Every head, men and women, in the restaurant turned as her loveliness sashayed past. Long blonde locks, which usually cascaded around her shoulders, were swept up in a glamorous bouffant hairstyle. Her black and white wardrobe was replaced for the night, by a stunning red, formfitting dress. Soft folds of it swished with each step around her perfect knees showing glimpses of toned legs above shapely calves. A thin waist was accentuated by full breasts, the dress's neckline left something to the imagination, making it even more alluring.

The effect had surely been strategically planned and the effort paid off. Seth was not sure any human male could resist her charms. He was prepared, even if he did not paint as striking a picture in his tailored gray suit and black button up shirt with open collar.

"Darling." Tillie greeted with a kiss on his cheek that would leave a lipstick mark. She was already branding her territory. "I have missed you so much. Your little experiment has stoked up the excitement, I can almost touch the electricity between us. We have so much to talk about. Who should go first?"

Yikes, they did have much to discuss, but not necessarily what Miss Morgan had in mind. He had planned to share his thoughts over dessert, but didn't want to lead her on during dinner. However, it felt the gentlemanly act to let the lady go first, not only because he was not ready, but Tillie may deal better with his news, if she had time to pour out her plans beforehand.

Seth could not have stopped the pre-planned onslaught even if he had attempted to. Tillie rushed right in before he had time to warn her, outlining her master assault on their future. He was barely able to sneak in a quick compliment. "Lovely ladies go first. And may I say you look even more ravishing than I remember, Till."

"That was the point Mister Hoffer." Tillie teased. "I have been a very busy girl, ready to make you one lucky guy. Would you like to hear about the apartment or wedding venue first?"

"Surprise me." This was not going to end well, unless he followed along with Tillie's plan and married a woman he had no business being with. How far would he go to keep the peace? But if he lost this battle, it would just be the beginning of the war.

"I will save the best for last... I put a refundable deposit on a penthouse unit in the One Dallas Center Luxury Apartments on Harwood. They are absolutely perfect. Modern open design, excellent views, even a bar, more for entertaining purposes since I know you're not much of a drinker. I was not sure if you would prefer a two or three bedroom, so it is a flexible deposit. It seems you are so excited you can barely speak?"

"Wow." Was about all Seth could rummage to the surface. If he married Tillie he would never need to make another plan the rest of his life, he would just jump in the car and go along for the bumpy ride.

"I know, I know...and that is not even the best part. I found the perfect place for our wedding. You are an old-fashioned, traditional kind of guy, this venue has elegance, charm and is even in a church for your religious mother. Have you heard of the Bell Tower Chapel and Gardens in Fort Worth? It will set a perfect backdrop for our lives together. The chapel was constructed with 1920's Neo Tudor-style architecture with a distinct steeple and working bell. It has cast stone arches and stunning stained glass. It will be like getting married in a fairytale...our own little castle surrounded by twenty acres of scenic gardens. I am so excited for you to see it. Unless you would prefer a destination wedding somewhere exotic?"

It was far worse than Seth had imagined and the worst part was that he had set himself up for the fall. Letting

Tillie go first made it impossible to get out of this gracefully.

"Wow again. All of this is so hard to believe. Let's eat and let the news settle over our meal and I will share my info with dessert. How's that?"

"Must be pretty sweet, I will let your news be my only dessert." Till obviously proud of herself with the analogy, didn't press for more.

Seth's food did not go down well and he could not come up with anything creative to take the sting off of his offering. Honesty would have to be the best policy and hopefully the least painful, like pulling off a Band-Aid quickly.

"Till, I am sorry, I did not come up with a more appealing profession for you in our six weeks apart. I enjoy what I do, for the most part, not some recent events maybe, and I think it is a worthwhile, maybe even meaningful way to provide a living."

"No problem sweetie, we still have time. I can always help you with that too. I have lots of ideas and connections. Seth Row has been a great place to make a name for yourself and will open many doors."

Seth was sure all she said was true and that was a large part of the problem. He felt castrated by her.

"Please wait Tillie, that is not all, it gets worse. A lot has transpired in six weeks, I found my dad and need to sort through some things that accompanied that knowledge.

You are the complete package for some lucky guy, but not me. Not now. And really, not ever."

He had spared her the part that absence had not made his heart grow fonder, but more absent. He had not really missed Tillie, much at all, and that was not a good sign. Tears filled her eyes, but did not spill over the mascaraed lashes. Seth was not sure if she was broken-hearted at the end of the relationship or just sad all her plans had been for naught.

He did feel compassion for the beautiful woman. He hated to hurt anyone. The way he had to look at this was that he was saving them both much pain later, after living years of a loveless or at least superficial relationship, built on non-eternal things. Tillie Morgan was rarely rattled and was able to compose herself quickly.

"I must admit, I am disappointed. I am rarely surprised by a man Seth. I think we could be a good team. I could make you the man you were meant to be Seth, regardless of who your parents are. I hope you don't regret this, because once I walk out of this restaurant, my ship has sailed and I will be moving on. Maybe still into One Dallas Center, it was pretty remarkable."

I, I, I…never we, which portrayed the problem in one tall, thin letter. She had not even asked anything about the identity of his father. She probably planned to make or re-create his identity as well. Tillie Morgan would always be okay and land on her manicured feet, because she had 'I'…herself….and Seth wanted to be a bigger part of the equation.

"I am incredibly sorry. Truly Tillie. I did not intend for things to go this way. I wish I could tell you differently, but I think us parting ways for now is for the best, for both of us. Your life will be incredible and amazing with or without me that is guaranteed. You deserve more."

To Tillie's credit, she did not dash from the room, but sat and calmly completed their time together at Wolfgang Puck's table. Perchance she was giving Seth a few last minutes to reconsider his dreadful mistake.

After he paid the check, they embraced one final time. The heat from her body warming him, but not arousing as it would most men. Things felt final. Tillie had not received The Bachelor's rose, but had been sent home. It was not the fairytale ending she had hoped for, but Seth felt relief with no regret.

That left girl number three. The one who did not even know she was in the running for the metaphoric rose on his imaginary Bachelor episode.

Seth gave Halle Valentine, psychic extraordinaire, a phone call and left her a message explaining he had had another paranormal incident and asking her to drop by when she could. He was not sure how to introduce the topic of enlisting her services as more than a psychic, best not even try to leave that on a voice message.

The next evening around nine o'clock P.M. Halle showed up. It had seemed longer then twenty-four hours as Seth impatiently waited. Her bouncy brown curls and personality warmed up the room. Seth immensely liked having her around. Her impact was immediate.

"I got your message and came as soon as I could. Took a chance you would be around tonight. What's new? Or how can I help?"

Seth wanted to blurt out that the way she could help was to date him. But he stayed in the safe lane by telling her what had been written in the mist on the shower door. That got a bigger reaction than if he had asked her out.

Halle gasped, "Your newbie is growing and getting better at communicating! How exciting. Who do you think he or she may be?"

"Not sure. Unfortunately, I know too many people that have been convicted as guilty in my line of work. It could be someone that was executed, who has returned to state his innocence, I suppose. Nearly half of those on death row still claim they did not do the crime they were convicted of at the time of execution, so that leaves a long list of possible shower buddies."

"I think you can limit it to those who lost their lives in the past few years, the spirit seems fairly fresh to his new state. I would also guess this one was younger when they passed on. The presence does not feel mature and I don't think they are done here. There is more they need to express, so be open and ready. I wish I could

179

just pull it out for you, but it is a process. I can stop by every few days and check on any new developments in their communication."

"That would be outstanding. Yes, please do," Seth answered, as he thought…yes, convenient, readymade dates.

More time with Halle was just what Seth wanted to work towards. He was not an impulsive man, but something about this, or her, made him feel like a teen again. Lyrics from The Chainsmokers and Cold Play's new song, "Something Just like This", came into his mind. Seth wondered if one of his phantom roommates was prodding him on.

The words fit what he was feeling…he was not looking for someone with superhuman gifts, even though Halle may have some. He was not a superhero and did not need a fairytale, but the line "Just someone I can turn to, somebody I can kiss", was exactly what he wanted. The line kept playing on repeat in his mind. Someone here must want him to kiss her or was he projecting his wishful thinking? He wanted the same thing, but wasn't ready. The words would not stop.

"Halle, there was one other item of business I needed to discuss with you…well not business really…you would not be paid for these services….that came out wrong…I know you don't perform those kind of services for money…dang…just… would you be willing to go on a real date with me?"

There he had said it, it was out of his mouth, but the lyrics of the song did not abate. "And I need to add that I think someone here wants me to kiss you. I know that sounds really weird. Sorry."

"Well, I must say that is the most unique pick up line I have ever had. Projecting your motives onto the unseen presences in the room I see. You are good, playing to a psych's weaknesses." Halle laughed. "But I am picking up matchmaking signals from your crew. I guess even the deceased need a little romance."

Who knew weirdness worked with some women? Halle was her own breed and this was the first time he wanted to thank his extraterrestrial tenants.

"I would hate to disappoint them. Who knows what they would do if we do not respond. It might help us communicate better with them too." Seth stretched, as he moved closer to Halle Valentine.

She did not move away, but appeared open to the idea. The pressure was on. He even had an audience.

Seth felt awkward as he moved in for the kiss, but the moment he took her smiling face gently in his hands, all awkwardness ended. Maybe the spirits intervened in his behalf, but it was the best first kiss, or any kiss, of his life. No thought went into the angling of their noses or opening and closing of eyes, things just fell delightfully into place. Soft, slightly open lips met and met and met as their kiss turned into kisses.

It was not an electric experience, there was no shock or pain involved. Magnetic was more the word he would use. Their lips connected as if pulled together and every time they parted, reconnected almost immediately. He would inhale her if he could. The connection of their lips seemed to connect their souls as well, he could feel every emotion she was feeling. Her psychic skills had been passed to him, like gum in the mouth transferred when French kissing. Eventually they had to take a breath and separated to take everything in.

"Whowziers! What was that!?"

"Well, I am an empath as you know and can pick up on other's emotions. My ability is often heightened when I touch the person I am reading. What I think happened, occasionally there are people that also receive emotions when touched by an empath. I believe you are one of those persons, Seth. As I was experiencing what you were feeling during our kiss, you could also feel my emotions in return. Double the pleasure you might say, but it can also double the sadness at times."

"That was incredible. I am going to enjoy kissing you…unless I end up receiving the impression that you do not feel pleasure during it. That would be a buzz-kill. May I officially ask you out on a date for this weekend? You can come read the room and then I will escort you beyond these walls."

"I would enjoy that. This relationship could get interesting. I need to go now, but will see you in the next couple days for sure."

Halle definitely 'received the rose' from Seth, the bachelor, this round. Just when he thought his life could not get any crazier, he gets romantic assistance from beyond the veil and finds he has return empath skills. Sort of like being a rare genetic match with your partner, but this wasn't for some exotic disease. Things could get fun determining the potential. A few days seemed like an eternity to wait to tap into Halle's emotions again.

The last female connection Seth made, in his estrogen fused few days, was a call to his mother. He just needed to hear Marion's voice telling him everything would be okay…even if it were not true.

He knew he would also need to tell her about the visit from his robed father. That was not a discussion he was looking forward to having with Marion. He hated to hurt her with the incredible story of her ex's continuing escapades. But he could do bad news/good news and end with telling her about his hook-up with Miss Halle Valentine. Leaving out a few of the more juicy nothing-mom-needs-to-know details, of course.

CHAPTER 17

Tying the knot or marriage is more common
on death row than one might think. In fact,
dozens of these services are performed yearly
in America alone. One difference between a
conventional ceremony and a death row
ceremony (other than the bleak environment
and the added chains) is the absence of the
words "till death do us part" in the vows. One
of the more famous cases of marriage is that
of Damien Wayne Echols and Lorri Davis. In
December 1999, Davis and Echols got married
in the Arkansas Penitentiary in a Buddhist
ceremony. They are still happily married
today, living in Salem. Echols was released on
an Alford plea after 18 years in prison. The
plea meant they had to admit that there was
enough evidence to find them guilty, but
enough mitigating factors to allow their
release—all the while maintaining their
innocence.

The next few weeks were some of the best of Seth's life,
despite the drama that was being played out around him.
Halle came by regularly to communicate with his
apartment dwellers and they even escaped on a few

dates. She was an easy breath of fresh air with empathetic lips. His mother liked her, his dog liked her, the relationship part of his life felt right for once.

However, that didn't erase the fact he was still dealing with one of the biggest dilemmas of his professional life at work. Today's Seth Row Radio Show was focused on Joshua and his impending execution. The team decided to hold the radio broadcast a week earlier than usual due to the fact they had not been able to figure out a way out of the execution episode and Seth wanted to give himself more than a few days to prepare, if he had to face that up front and center.

The callers, so far, had not been gentle in their opinions, using the words twisted, demonic, con-kid, sadistic, etcetera, to describe the incarcerated teen. Seth was just waiting for a mob to call in chanting *'Crucify him, crucify him'*! His listeners were already crucifying the young inmate verbally.

Megan from Des Moines just expressed that Joshua was a fake and a brutal boy, trying to draw sympathy due to his age, he deserved to die and she would be happy to watch it happen. Ouch. When did his female fans get so barbaric? He could picture a group of agitators storming the studio with pitch forks, like the scene from *Beauty and the Beast* when they were going after the Beast yelling *'get the Beast, get the Beast'*. It was probably good Joshua was safe behind bars. Seth thanked Megan for her call and picked up the line with Felicity from Twin Falls.

"I wasn't going to call in, but I cannot listen to this tirade against a decent young man any longer."

"Felicity, thank you for your call. It will be refreshing to have an opposing opinion. Why do you think Joshua is a decent human being and not the demon he has been portrayed?"

"Well for one, my daughter attended the same school Joshua did, St. Edwards, for a few years and he rescued her from bullies."

"Would you be willing to share more details of what happened with our listeners?"

"I will try to, to the best of my memory. It has been three to four years ago now. My daughter Becca was not a popular girl at the school. We did not have a lot of money, like many of the student's families who go there, we enrolled her at St. Edwards for religious reasons. Even though the students wore uniforms, she was sometimes teased about her clothes and the way she wore her hair. Little things, nothing major, we just told her it was the others, not her, and she would have to deal with those kind of people her whole life.

Then one day a few of the most obnoxious boys drug her into the boy's bathroom. I am not sure what they planned to do with her in there…beat on her, heaven forbid, abuse her, or maybe just embarrass and scare her. Luckily we never had to find out, because Joshua came in after them. He was tall for his age, but not strongly built, he could not have taken on all three physically, but Becca said he never intended to fight them."

"What happened then? What did he do?" Seth pried.

"In Becca's words, he just looked at them with staring eyes. She said everything got very quiet. The biggest boy asked if he planned to rat on them. Joshua said no, but he had a message for them. The boys were still acting all bravado and tough, but asked him what the message was. Joshua told them he knew from a higher source, or something like that, whatever they chose to do to Becca would be acted out upon each of them in the days to come, if they proceeded."

"Doesn't that just show or prove he was violent?" Seth interrupted.

"No, you don't understand, Joshua was not saying he was the one going to exact the punishment, only witnessing that it would come. He was a gentle soul. Always kind to the underdog when we knew him. I know people can change, but I would be shocked if he changed that much."

"So what did the gang do?" Seth continued.

"They let Becca go, scoffing they never planned to do anything anyway, just scare her. We transferred Becca to a public school not long after the incident, but I did hear that something unpleasant happened to each of those boys before the end of the year. Joshua was not involved in any of the abuses, but he predicted them."

"You do not think Joshua caused bad things to happen to the other boys?"

"No, I am sure not. But there is something different about him. He is in tune with things most of us are not. I would hesitate to be maligning him, like your other callers."

"Thanks for your input Felicity."

Seth was having trouble being objective with this one. Maybe he should just tell Brin Gillette that Joshua was his brother and asked to be recused, due to conflict of interest or blood. He was just not ready to share their linked lineage with the world yet. He could foresee, even without possession of special gifts, that information would unleash a media frenzy which would not be pretty for any of them. He wished he had foresight like his half-brother or could read the room like his gal pal. He could not do this right now. He was done.

Seth found a song, "Bittersweet Symphony" seemed appropriate, to play over the air while he looked for a sound clip from one of Texas's senators discussing the laws on the death penalty. When the senator's voice began to drone on, Seth walked out of the sound booth. He knew the recorded interview lasted for twenty minutes, so would fill the rest of his air time. What was he going to do?

Bear accosted him before he could get out the door.

"Where's the fire boss? Need some help?"

"Gees Bear… you startled me. I just needed some air, off the air, before I meltdown. This one is far too close. I cannot get a handle on it. Do you think the guy is guilty? Tell me what to do."

"What do you want to do, Seth?"

"What do I want to do? I want to go get mitts and a baseball and play a round of catch with the guy, maybe throw a three-way triangle with the priest too, and get to know my family members, away from all this ugly. It is too late for what I want to do. What I don't want to do is watch Josh get executed and not be able to do a thing about it. This just sucks."

"Our lawyers say you are bound by contract to host the show if the network wants it. Sorry my friend, their paperwork is ironclad. I haven't been able to talk Brin G. or the NBC gargantuans out of the idea either. Let's focus on getting the governor to extent the time, which might be our best hope at this point. What do you think?"

"I think I am going to go call my sister. Could you close the show for me?"

Seth wandered out onto the sidewalk and dialed the number to St. Edwards School in Twin Falls, Idaho. Mother Mary Catherine answered the phone.

"Could I please speak with Postulate Eliza Marie? This is Seth Hoffer. It is very important."

"Eliza Marie is in noviiiate classes right now, may I take a message for her?"

"No message, it is vital I talk to her. I promised. Please have compassion on me Mother Mary. I can wait for you to get her." Seth sounded a bit over-dramatic even to himself.

"Hold on," was the brief reply and then Seth heard steps shuffling away from the phone. Before too long a meek, "hello" came across the phone line.

"Is this Eliza Marie? If so, I have a message for you."

"Yes, I am Sister Eliza Marie. Who would give me a message?" The voice was not much more than a whisper, young and sweet sounding.

'My name is Seth Hoffer. I promised your brother to tell you something."

After an audible gasp on the other end, Seth proceeded to share with Eliza Marie the information he told her brother. He had seen their birth certificate, their mother had died giving birth. She had not abandoned them and he was sure she loved them both dearly.

"My mother was named Eliza Marie too? And she studied to be a nun before I was born? Soft weeping could be heard through his receiver.

"I am so sorry. I wish I had better news for you."

"No, thank you. This is wonderful news. I feel connected to her somehow. Maybe she is watching over us from heaven. Did you find out anything about our father?"

"Not yet," Seth lied to the nearly-nun upon making a swift decision to spare pain rather than be totally forthcoming, and that news should come from the Father, "but I am working on it."

"Bless you Mr. Hoffer. May I ask for one more favor? Can you do anything to help my brother?"

"I am working on that too Eliza, but it doesn't look good. Telling you about your mother and not sharing your identity with the media were his greatest concerns."

"Yes, Josh is like that, always thinking of others first. Please let him know how much I love him and I pray for him many times a day. One of the perks of studying to become a nun, lots of prayer time."

"I will pass along your return message to him for sure. Anything else?" Seth wanted to hug the frail girl, through the phone. He wished he could tell her she had another brother closer than she knew and a father, who was a Father, right next to her, but it was not the time.

"Not for now. Does Mother Mary Catherine have your number should I need to get in contact?"

"Not sure, I will leave it with you, or her. And please do call if you think of anything I can do."

The call ended before Seth was ready, but he could not think of any reason to keep her on the phone, without admitting he just wanted to get to know his half-sister better. Now he was the one who felt like crying. He had kept his promise to Joshua at least and needed to careful not to put the press on to Eliza Marie's scent. A seventeen year old twin sister of a convicted murderer on death row was big news. If he wasn't going to get to interview her, no one was.

CHAPTER 18

Members of the media are allowed to witness
executions, divided equally as possible
between the rooms containing the offender's
and victim's witnesses. A representative of the
Associated Press is guaranteed one of the five
slots. Other media members must submit
their requests at least three days prior to the
execution date; priority is given to media
members representing the area in which the
capital crime took place. The Huntsville Item
(the local newspaper for Huntsville, Texas)
generally covers all executions, regardless of
county of conviction. Generally, other
newspapers will only cover executions where
the crime was committed within their general
circulation area. College and university media
are not permitted to be witnesses.

Seth didn't feel like going back into the studio after
Eliza's call. He wandered aimlessly for a while until he
realized he was heading in the direction of his mother's
house. He started to jog, then run, it felt good. He
probably should have put on running shoes or workout
clothes, but he didn't care what people thought. It might
add interest to passers-by pondering his plight, a

business-dressed man running down the road. He didn't care if he was recognized.

Even the car parked in the driveway on Wildflower Way, did not deter him from barging through his mother's door. But he took a step back, when he realized Raul Valentine was seated at his mother's table, like he belonged there. Seth was nearly positive his mother was not having a paranormal incident, so what in the world was going on?

"Seth, what a nice surprise." Then noticing his sweaty, unkempt appearance and crazed look… "Why do you look like you are strung out on drugs? Oh, and I believe you know Mr. Valentine."

"I am not on drugs Ma, I just ran over here from work. I wanted to talk to you, but I'll come back at a less-busy time. I did not know you had company."

"Raul and I were just finishing lunch, you are welcome to stay."

Raul, perhaps picking up on psychic vibes or at least somewhat socially aware, added to Marion's words, "In fact, I am just going to take off. Say hello to that girl of mine for me. Hope she is giving you good service, she seems to be over at your place a lot lately."

"Halle has been very helpful. Thank you. Don't leave on my account."

"No, its fine, I'll be back later." Raul stood up to go, but leaned in and gave his mother a peck on the check before exiting.

Was Seth's whole world inside out? No wonder his mother had taken the news about Sam so well. She had finally moved on, and he could not fault her for being attracted to a Valentine. The whole double-dating with family members was just a little awkward. He didn't want to begrudge Marion a little happiness - but did it have to be with Halle's father?

After Raul departed, Seth said, "Mom, you could have given me a heads up."

"Looks who's talking, Mr. Burst-through-the-door. I didn't say anything, because I didn't want it to cause any issues between you and Halle. You seem so happy with her. Raul and I are just enjoying each other's company and seeing where things go. We were both lonely. Enough about me, you must have something important to share to run a marathon in your suit?"

"I need some advice, from someone I trust, mom. So much has been happening lately, my head is swimming with information I cannot seem to sort through rationally. Maybe you can help me put things in order. Just saying it out loud may help."

Marion listened as Seth dumped out the rest of the recent events in his life, making a messy pile of info on the table between them which was already covered with dirty dishes. He added on to the story of Father

Brogan's visit (which she knew about), the tale that he also has twin half-siblings, who are not aware they all share a father. The girl is a secret and becoming a nun. The boy happens to be the young man currently on death row and the inmate of focus on his show. His network wants him to do a live execution broadcast and to make it all worse, he is pretty sure Joshua, the boy, is not guilty. That about sums it up, besides the supernatural events in his apartment. Marion did not interrupt with the million questions that filled her brain, but sat patiently waiting for he son to get it all out and empty the baggage he was carrying.

"Whoa son, heavy load. Let's take one thing at a time to determine what you can do something about and what you will just have to ride out. What is burdening you the most at this moment?"

"I am battling a moral dilemma, mom. I am not sure I can, in good conscience, host a live execution. Especially one of a possible half-brother. But, I am legally bound to do it. It just feels so wrong and gratuitous. If I don't do it, I could be fired or worse, sued. If I do, do it, I am not sure I can live with myself. But, if it is going to be done regardless, I wouldn't want anyone else putting Joshua through difficult questions, trapping him, or mocking him. I don't want him to face death alone."

"From what I hear, it sounds like you know what you need to do. When we care about someone, we are willing to do hard things for them, so they don't have to suffer. You cannot take away this boy's burden, but it sounds like you can help him carry it. I am proud of you Seth,"

Seth had not seen it from that perspective before. It was a sacrifice to do something he abhorred. But if he could save Joshua one ounce of pain, he could do it, he wanted to do it.

He felt a bit better, enough to eat one of his mom's left-over chicken salad sandwiches on a crescent roll with a bowl of her homemade vegetable soup. He thanked his mother and gave her a long hug, before he left, both physically and emotionally fed.

Out in front of her house on the sidewalk, Seth realized that he did not have a car. He walked to the corner and called an Uber to take him to his vehicle. Feeling much relief, but still not wanting to be alone, he dialed Halle's number and left a message requesting her services for the evening, in whatever capacity she was available...as a psychic, girlfriend, or daughter of his mother's beau. He smiled imagining her listening to it.

Halle didn't return his call, but arrived an hour or so after Seth got home. Barney Fife was sitting beside him on the couch, front paws across Seth's legs, licking his hand and sporadically the side of his face when Halle walked in.

"Tough day? Scoot over Barney-boy, I can take it from here." She slid in beside Seth on the sofa. "I came as soon as I heard your message. I'm available for number one, two or three, host's choice."

"I can probably use all three tonight. Just sit with me for a few minutes and then let's see if you can get any more info out of the dead guys hanging out here. I could really use any insights they have to give ASAP."

"The energy in this room is off the charts tonight. Someone wants to communicate so badly they are about to explode." Halle picked up Seth's saliva-coated hand and held it in her lap.

They sat in silence. Anxiety erupting from his fingers and diffusing slightly as it flowed through hers. They really needed a breakthrough tonight, before Seth had a breakdown. She could feel the multiple emotions he was experiencing without him saying a word. Peace back-flowed into Seth from the grounded girl beside him. She didn't have to say things would be okay, she believed they would. It helped him hope too.

Daylight dissipated into dusk as they sat. Occasionally Seth would verbalize his pressing concerns, which Halle already sensed, but vocalizing the words washed them away as well. Before complete darkness, Halle whispered in Seth's ear. "Do you see what I am seeing?"

Seth's eyes scanned the room. His senses were enhanced from Halle's nearness. Across the room was a faint glow that was ebbing and flowing. The shape was not static, but verged on a human form, almost a hologram, only with less density.

"Is that a person?"

'I think it's our young friend. He is trying so hard to communicate with us, he has worked up a spiritual sweat of sorts. We can see his essence from all the energy expended. I don't want to scare him away, but I need to get closer."

Halle dropped the dryer, calmer hand back onto Seth's lap and glided across the room next to the apparition. She was so close she could touch him and then she was amidst him. Seth swallowed a shriek. What was she doing!? The two forms, translucent and opaque, overlapped as one. That is one way to communicate, the ultimate mind-meld, Seth thought. He was frozen in place on his fabric furniture. Halle began to put into words what she was comprehending mingled with the presence.

"I am not picking up a name...just John Doe...I think he wants to remain anonymous."

"No, Halle, there is a John Doe, Jonny Doe. The boy Joshua supposedly murdered."

The power surge was so strong Halle was almost knocked to the floor. "I think you deciphered the identity of our unknown, Seth. I think this is Jonny. Welcome Jonny. You are among friends. But he is disagreeing about Joshua murdering him. Did you leave Seth the message? Did you write 'not guilty' in Latin on the shower door?"

Jonny's presence grew more intense. Halle continued. "I can sense powerful love in the room. Jonny you love Joshua...like a brother....and there is another brother? Does that make sense Seth?"

"More than you know. Ask if Joshua did not do it, who did?"

"It doesn't work quite like that, but I will see what I can feel." Halle was so still for a few moments Seth wondered if she had fallen asleep standing up. Jonny's light combined and separated, eerily intimate, with his girlfriend. "I am picking up the letter T. Does that mean anything to you?"

"Oh, gosh no, Sam's middle initial is a T. Please don't let it be him."

"I am not getting positive energy in response to that name. There was another man in the park with them that night. Professional or from a profession nearby maybe?

"Profession nearby? That leaves, librarian, mortician, policeman or priest. Take your pick. Or there were homeless there at times too."

"Not homeless, but I think from one of the other four categories. T. is still coming strongly. Trumble or Treadman or Truman...Seth, maybe Google some of these last names in conjunction with Twin Falls. See if any there are any matches with T. names that might work in one of the businesses around the park. Jonny

202

you are doing so well. I am proud of you. We want to help. Anything else?"

Halle was good at pausing to give Jonny time to express himself. Seth didn't know if he could be as patient. He wanted to shake the information out of the boneless boy...gently of course. Halle continued reflecting what she thought she received.

"Joshua came to help? Seth, I think Joshua was abused by the same man. He left to escape it, but returned when he knew Jonny was in trouble, Jonny had taken his place. Oh, Jonny we are so sorry he did not make it in time."

The light that was Jonny almost burst into flame, then slowly subdued until it was barely visible.

Halle collapsed on the floor in exhaustion. Seth sprinted the few feet to her side, scooped her up into his arms, cradling her on his lap. He could feel she was depleted, but content and happy. He put his chin on Halle's curly head and waited a while for her to recover.

Halle finally roused, but was still groggy and unable to carry on a continuous conversation. Seth laid her gently on the couch with a pillow, blanket and deputy dog on guard by her feet. He pulled out his laptop to focus on finding this letter T. guy, while Halle recovered her strength.

Seth first looked at all the T.'s associated with St. Edwards finding only, Helene Teresa, not likely a nun, and his father's middle initial. He jotted down the two names and headed clockwise around the park to the business on the east, Twin Falls Public Library. There were over ten employees who worked at the library full or part-time. There was a Tara, first name, and Tueller, last name, but both were women. Only two men were listed and the only T. name was a Theodore Mundy, who appeared to be well over sixty in his photo and about as virile as a boiled noodle. Seth knew looks could be deceiving, but he had his doubts on this old guy having the strength to overpower a tiny kitten, let alone a teenage male.

The Mortuary had fifteen names on their website, but even though in the business of death, there was not one T. on the whole list. They were easy to dismiss. That left the County Jail and Courthouse on the west side. It was a little more difficult to maneuver their website to find all listed on the county payroll.

The captain's name was Tony Miller and a Tim Paxton was one of the officers who patrolled a beat around town. The last T. name he found was a Detective Thomas Truman. This guy also volunteered to serve over the Court Appointed Special Advocates that according to the information provided online, "support and promote abused or neglected children in order to provide children with a safe environment in permanent homes. In many jurisdictions the CASA are known as Guardians as litem".

The hair on the back of Seth's neck stood on end like Barney's did when he sensed danger and chills went through his whole body. This guy had complete access to the guardian-less kids who lived at St. Edwards. He was in a position to assist in providing a safe environment. A true wolf in sheep's clothing prowling in their midst. There was no photo, but with the double T. name and his heart pounding in his chest, Seth had an idea this could be their man. He went over to Halle and put his hand lightly on her shoulder. Her eyes opened and she looked lucid.

"Hals, I know you are beat, but what impressions do you get from the name, Tom Truman?

Her body tensed noticeably under his touch and she shuddered. There was even a buzz of energy from the location Seth had last semi-seen Jonny across the room.

"I will take that as an indication you both feel this could be the perp. Now the bad news. He works for the police department and our only evidence against him is from a dead boy and a psychic reader, which could propose a problem."

"But Seth, we have to do something."

"Don't worry, I will. I plan to get together with Bear first thing in the morning and contact the governor's office to request a stay of execution for Joshua. At least until they can evaluate the new evidence we have discovered."

"On what grounds? A spirit appeared to your psychic girlfriend? They may find those facts questionable."

"No, how about ...I have received new evidence from a witness who would like to remain anonymous. Sounds better than... has to remain anonymous, or at least invisible, because he is dead. I think I may get some journalistic leeway with an 'anonymous source' who fears for their life. It is all we've got and we need to try.

And a shout out to all you here from the other side, you'll need to help too. Jonny, Amos and anyone else, maybe you can send some buddies over to influence the Gov? We are all on this mission together. Huddle, fist pump and let's go team!" Seth was always Seth, even in a crisis.

CHAPTER 19

Defendants can seek judicial review of the sentence and also appeal to the Texas Board of Pardons and Paroles for commutation of the sentence to life in prison. The Board, after hearing testimony, decides whether or not to recommend commutation to the Governor of Texas. If the Board recommends commutation, the Governor can accept or reject the recommendation. However, if the board does not recommend commutation, the Governor has no power to override the Board's nonrecommendation (the law was changed in 1936 due to concerns that pardons were being sold for cash under the administrations of former Governor James E. Ferguson and later his wife and Texas's first female Governor Miriam A. Ferguson). The only unilateral action which the Governor can take is to grant a one-time, 30 day reprieve to the defendant, and can do so regardless of what the Board recommends in a particular case. Since Texas reinstated the death penalty in 1976, only two defendants sentenced to death have been granted clemency by the Governor after a recommendation from the Board.

Early the next morning, Bear helped Seth prepare the paperwork for the stay of execution and drove it to the governor's office himself. It was a last ditch effort, another Hail Mary, but Bear did some of his best work when the odds were not in his favor. He was the go-to guy to get things done under impossible odds and it was cathartic for Bear to be able to assist his struggling friend in some way.

Time was of the essence. They had less than forty-eight hours. The Seth Row Special starring Joshua was tomorrow tonight and his execution scheduled for the morning after. Bear would put on the full court press if needed. Governor's office beware.

Seth left Halle asleep on his couch when he went to meet Bear at dawn in their offices. She was conked out, still depleted from her emotional expenditure the night before. He was heading back home to check on her when his cell phone buzzed. An unfamiliar number scrolled across the screen.

Seth pulled over to take the call, he wanted to be safe, both with his driving and by not missing any important communication. Who knew who could be on the other end of the line, considering all the unusual events taking place in his world currently?

A soft female voice asked, "Is this Seth, the Seth in Texas who called with a message from my brother Josh?"

Seth was so relieved he had picked up the anonymous call. "Yes, yes, this is me, Seth in Texas. I am so glad to hear your voice Eliza. How can I help you?"

"I am not sure if you can, but I had to talk to someone. I know it would upset Joshua if I came there. It means so much to him to keep me safe, removed from all of his drama, but I cannot stand it. How is he? What can I do? Is he really going to die?" Sobs could be heard coming through the phone from far away in Idaho. Seth wished he could hug his baby sister, but a cyber-hug would have to do right now.

"Eliza, I wish I could say all you want to hear. I am doing all I can down here. There is a chance, a very small one mind you, but a glimmer of hope, that we might be able to save your brother. Gather all the nuns you know and any other believers-in-a-higher-power that you can and start praying. We have uncovered some new information from a reliable source and have appealed to the governor for a stay of execution to have time to follow up on the leads."

"I have been pleading for heaven's help already, but I will include or ask others to join in as well. Officer Truman is waiting outside Mother Mary Catherine's office for me right now. I am going to see if there is anything he can do for Josh too." Eliza shared.

Seth's heart started pounding so hard it was as if it was trying to beat a hole through his chest wall.

"Eliza, listen to me. This is vital. Do not meet up with Officer Truman. Please, I insist, at least for a few days or until you hear back from me."

"But Mr. Seth. He is outside the door waiting for me right now."

"Make any excuse you can think of, or if you cannot tell a little fib, slip out the back way or through a window if you have to. Just trust me." Seth could feel perspiration on his brow.

"Why? You are scaring me. I just want to help Joshua."

Seth could hear more tears. "I promise Eliza, this is the best way you can help him right now. I care about you more than you understand. We need to talk further and will soon. You have more family than you know. But right now, just go, make yourself scarce, avoid Officer Truman and I will call you as soon as I know more. Can you do that for me?"

"I will try my best…. just help Josh…" And Eliza was gone.

Seth tried not to panic. He did not want or need another crisis to deal with. Hopefully the governor's office would have someone all over the Tom Truman situation in the very near future.

Instead of driving straight home, Seth swung by his mother's house again, he was not really sure why, but it was always a safe place to land and get out of the quagmire for a minute. Seth was not a kid anymore, he shouldn't need warm milk and cookies to feel better, but his car was taking him to Marion's despite that fact.

"Hey mom, I just need quick a hug," were the words that fell from out of Seth's mouth as he ambled through the door on Wildflower. Mother's arms opened to receive her son and Seth dropped his head onto her shoulder and let his tears spill down her back. He needed to get his emotions under control, so he could be strong by the time he got home to Halle, he was not ready to appear weak in front of her. Who was he kidding, with her skills she knew exactly who he was.

"What can I do for you my sad or very stressed son?" Marion had not seen Seth this vulnerable since he was ten.

"You are doing it mom. But maybe one more favor?"

"Just name it, you know I am here for anything you need…within reason of course."

"Will you come to Joshua's execution? Not to watch, just to be there in case I crumble. You can even see Sam…not to reconcile or anything. He is totally committed to the priest gig, just maybe for some closure for you both. This family needs some healing."

"Well, I must say, I was not expecting that at all. That is a request and then some." Marion responded, knowing she was willing to help her son in any way possible.

"It would mean a lot to me, mom."

"Of course, I will be there then. Let's hope there will be no execution to witness, shall we…unless it is me killing your father after all these years. Just jesting, just jesting, Seth. Mostly."

Seth could see where his unflappable and at times verging on inappropriate sense of humor came from. Sam was not very funny. The Marion pit-stop was a rapid release valve for some of his exploding pressure. Seth left the parental homestead a little lighter.

He finally returned home to find Halle recovered and just getting ready to leave.

"No, I have not moved in Seth, I am on my way out, but what a night! Do you have any good news before I go?" Halle asked.

"Where to begin, let's see…Bear is presently wrestling with the governor to save a life, my little sister is trying to outwit and outrun an incognito child molester and murderer, while I am planning a little family reunion at the execution. Just a normal day in the life of Seth Hoffer." Seth's adrenaline was pumping. "Can you come down with the team to Joshua's TV Special tomorrow night? I think it would be nice to have a psychic there to read the proceedings."

"So I would be attending in an official capacity?"

"More like doing double duty or fulfilling two roles at one time, if you can handle it"

"Of course I'll come. I get the feeling Jonny plans to be there too. He may be of assistance. Not that you could stop him from going anyway."

"Wonder how Jonny boy would look on camera? I have a feeling this is going to be the strangest show yet. I think I can get through tomorrow's interview. Just not sure about the following show, when Josh walks the proverbial plank." Seth's mood became more ponderous.

"Let's hope it won't come to that Seth. We'll save Joshua, we've got to. And we have secret weapons no one expects, human and spiritual beings working toward this goal from two dimensions. The fates are on our side," Halle rallied. "Oh, and can I ride with the team tomorrow or should I meet you in Huntsville?"

"Assuming I can get you clearance Halle, meet us at the studio tomorrow at noon. You can ride to the prison with Bear and I, or in the van with the team if you prefer. Jonny can find his own way."

"Hang in there Seth. You've got this. I'll see you at noon tomorrow."

He wanted to ask for another kiss before she took off. He needed to test that whole empath receiver thing again, but it didn't feel like the right time. Seth settled for a warm goodbye embrace. Their chests pressed together was not as powerful a connection as the sensitive lip sensors had been, but he was still picking up Halle had more humming around inside her that she had not shared.

"Hey, I have left you alone in this open-veil-vortex, is there anything else I should know before I let you go?" Seth whispered in Halle's ear as he pulled her closer.

"You have been dealing with so much Seth, I didn't know if you wanted more to process. I did pick up some new communications if you are interested."

"Why stop now, lay them on me. I may not want to know everything, but I need to at this point. Please proceed to enlighten me." Seth pulled away, but took Halle's hands in his so he could look into her brown eyes with golden sparkles as she spoke.

"Well, I believe the family member that is here watching over you is named Marvin. Does that make any sense to you? He is quite a crusty, but classy gentleman. You would like him."

"He would be my mother's father. Wow, welcome to grandpa Marv. Anything else?"

"For some reason it appears part of Saint Patrick's clan is gathering as well. You don't happen to be Irish, do you Seth?"

"My father was or is Irish and always insisted he was related to the Saint. I guess he was right. Ha-ha we have backup from both sides of the fam. My place must be getting pretty congested in the spirit realm, I may need to add on an extra wing or get a bigger place." Seth did not feel at all overwhelmed by the invisible family reunion. He felt strengthened by the see-through army. "Should I be nervous or do anything?"

"Nope, they've got things under control and will do what they can to help you and Joshua. Just stay out of their way and enjoy their company if possible. That's all I know."

And with that, Halle gave Seth an impish grin and was gone.

Hopefully they would have plenty of time to experiment on his and Halle's empath connection in the near future. Preferably without so many witnesses observing in his apartment and minus the taste of imminent death in his mouth.

Seth sat in his broken down leather chair feeling a bit broken himself. Barney and the other guys were around too…Jonny, Amos, Gpa Marv, and who knows how many of the Brogan bunch. Of course he only could see and touch the dog, but he was quite aware the two of them were not alone.

"Jonny thanks for not giving up on me. I will do my best to save your friend. Amos, I suppose I should feel honored you trusted me enough to take up residence. And to anyone else here, I appreciate you not haunting the place. If you have any inspirations for me, prod me along. If not, please go find someone somewhere else to enlist in this fight.

Oh, and if Joshua does die, God forbid, please bring him here to live with us too."

CHAPTER 20

Upon the offender's death the body is immediately embalmed, and disposed of in one of the following ways:

*A relative or bona fide friend of the offender may demand or request the body within 48 hours after death, upon payment of a fee not to exceed US$25 for the mortician's services in embalming the deceased.

*If no relative or bona fide friend requests the body, the Anatomical Board of the State of Texas may request the body, but must also pay the US$25 fee for embalming services.

*If no relative, bona fide friend, or the Anatomical Board requests the body, the body shall be "decently buried" with the embalming fee to be paid by the county.

The TDCJ (Texas Department of Criminal Justice) keeps an online record of all of its executions, including race, age, county of origin, and last words. The TDCJ is the only corrections agency in the US to extensively catalog the last words of executed inmates, and the only one to post the last words other than California. The main TDCJ prison cemetery for prisoners not picked up by their families after death is the Captain Joe Byrd Cemetery in Huntsville. Headstones of death row prisoners have prison numbers with the beginning "999", a state designation for a death row inmate, or they have the letters "EX" or "X".

Tomorrow arrived with anticipation spiking in the air. As the team readied for Joshua's Seth Row Special a cloud of death hung over Seth, its suffocating presence felt like he was preparing for his own execution, instead of his brother's. The room where they shot the show felt like a crypt.

He had at least gotten ahold of Sister or Mother Mary Catherine, he had enough trouble keeping his family tree accurate let alone all the Catholics. She had assured him Eliza Marie was fine and they were taking good care of her. He did not share with this other-mother the nature of his concern. Seth was semi-optimistic that Bear's persuasive powers worked their magic on those state guys and an investigation was under way…less than twenty-four hours remained ticking on death row's clock.

Jake, Joey and Gun respectively indicated they were ready and Bear voiced that it was time to start the show. These guys really were the best co-workers and friends a man could have. What a team these Row-bots had become. They had supported him through everything and actually accepted his ghost story. He would like to think he would do the same for each of them. Seth took a deep breath and said a micro-prayer in his mind. It was never too late to start praying.

They aired some pre-shot footage and clips from the trial before Joshua was led into the area and seated at the table across from Seth for the live interview portion of the special. This young man was not like any other prisoner Seth had ever interviewed. More than that, he was not like any person he had ever known, inside prison or out. And not just because the condemned man was his half-brother.

He was aloof, detached, separated or elevated from it all, not in an arrogant way. It was almost as if he did not care whether he lived or died. But what happened did matter to Seth.

As Seth observed the teen, he was more than convinced Sam had fathered Joshua too. The little similarities he had not noticed before glaringly stood out now. The way Joshua held his hands with fingers interlaced and rolled his thumbs, the cocked angle of his head with strong defiant jawline.

The pale green-gray eyes peering out of stubbled face. It was like Seth was looking at a younger version of himself in the mirror. A more handsome, more together, version of himself possibly, despite the fact the boy was wearing an orange jumpsuit and chains. Seth wondered if the television viewers could see the resemblance, it did not seem they could miss it, but he had.

Halle had come along, she was waiting just outside the production area for moral support and psychic intervention if needed. If the execution proceeded to take place in the morning, his mother would be there too. Father Brogan called and requested to be in attendance. Seth feared the priest would not arrive in time if he traveled by bus again. So, though he had not totally forgiven the man, Seth sprung for Sam's flight for Joshua's sake. Josh's father and Father both needed to be there, the fact they shared the same body saved Seth an extra ticket.

He did not even know what to ask in the interview. Seth just wanted to have a heart-to-heart with his little brother. He wanted to know everything about him before it was too late, before he was gone…perhaps Josh would come visit the apartment too and hang out with the other dead guys there who had also passed (partially) on. Even his usual attempt at levity was not helping relieve his stress.

Seth felt frantic, he was not his normal self-composed self. For the first time, he knew the man before him was innocent and it made the interview an unbearable mockery. His stomach felt sick and he was getting a stress headache, but the show must go on.

The young prisoner across from him looked as cool a cucumber…sheesh, what did that even mean, enough metaphors… Joshua just looked calm and at peace. Seth hoped he did too, for the cameras at least.

"How are you this evening Joshua? I am aware there is a last minute appeal for a pardon, or at least a stay of execution in your behalf, resulting from some new evidence. Do you feel hopeful?"

"There is always hope, but whether I live less than twenty-four more hours, or twenty-four more years, does not really matter. It is more about what you do with the time you have been given here."

"Do you feel, at only seventeen years old, like you have had enough time?"

"There is never enough time for those here on earth, but where I am going time is not measured, it is of no consequence."

"Is there anything you will miss?"

"There is one thing, or person, but I would prefer not to share their identity at this time. I believe I will also miss you Seth, my brother, you have been fair and kind to me. I guess I will miss all things good."

The "my brother" comment caught Seth off guard. Did Joshua sense their relationship? Or was it more "my brother" in the generic meaning that we are all brothers and sisters in God's family? Seth wanted to tell him they were brothers, that they shared the same father. Did he dare? Seth decided to wander off-script and see where it took him.

"For the record, I want you to know that I do believe in your innocence Joshua. Something I have never felt or expressed in any other of my Seth Row Specials."

"You are a good man Seth, even though I know at times you doubt that you are. This world needs more men like you. You are on the right track. Life is a journey, we mortals usually cannot see the end as clearly as I can at this junction, but must do the best we can each day until it arrives. Perhaps a short life is easier."

"How can you be so calm?" Suddenly Seth was not just wandering, he had jumped the tracks, "Jonny spoke to us, I know you were trying to help him. He may even be here now." Seth had gone completely off the rails with this sharp turn. Jonny was dead. He had just admitted 'on air' to be communicating with departed spirits. He dared not share he also had an idea who did commit the crime in case it enabled Mr. Truman to cover his tracks.

"Yes, I can feel Jonny's presence here with us," Joshua spoke with his eyes closed, slowly opening them, he looked around the room and added, "the line between our two worlds is quite thin for me at this junction and it seems Jonny brought an Irish army with him for some reason. It is not that kind of fight my dearest friend, my most loyal Jon." Then turning back to Seth, "He would make an effort to do anything he could for me. I wish it had been me instead of him in that park. I would have willingly died in his place. I do look forward to seeing him again…dwelling in the same dimension."

Seth was just waiting for Jonny to make his film debut any minute and start glowing for the camera. It was too bad Sam had not arrived yet to hang out with his clansman, or were clansman only Scottish? Anyway, he may have to call in Halle as interpreter or at least referee for his audience soon. He did not speak 'spirit' as fluently as she did. Maybe they could do a supernatural-style interview with dual hosts, sort of a séance with lights.

Seth continued on with the death row special as if all of this was totally routine, "I understand that. I think I would be willing to die in your place Joshua. I truly am your brother."

Would he really? Was that true or did he say it for dramatic effect? No, Seth knew in his heart it was true. He would be willing to give his life for this little brother. What a mind-blowing revelation. At that moment Seth wanted more than anything, for Joshua to know they were truly brothers by blood.

He did not want Joshua to leave this world not knowing. He knew his audience would not understand, they would just think he was speaking in the metaphoric sense. He hoped somehow Joshua knew. He wanted to shout, I really am your brother. Father Brogan actually begat both of us.

"I believe you are sincere, Seth. But that will not be asked of you. Just the one request I gave you previously is enough."

"I have done what you asked, but want to do more."

What more could he do? He would whisper in Joshua's ear when they were off camera their biological connection. To hell, literally, with Father Brogan, he wanted his brother to know. Hopefully it would give him more peace than pain. In reality, the peace was for himself, Joshua had already arrived on that plain. But at least Joshua would know that Eliza would still have family that cared for her when he was gone. If he was gone.

"Please don't sorrow over me Seth. Death is what gives life meaning. If this precious commodity of earth life was endless, it would not be such a treasure. We value it because of its brevity. And where this life is pain, we are comforted that there will be an end to our suffering one day and it will not go on forever. The hardest part is leaving behind those we love or in worrying how much we will be missed. Fortunately, very few will miss me when I am gone." Joshua revealed.

"I will. And now that America is getting to know you, I believe they will as well." And if you do leave us, it looks like you have an army of kinsmen waiting just on the other side, Seth almost added.

Now Seth was clinging on with his fingertips. He prayed again, twice now today, and he had not prayed anything in a very long time. This time he asked that the governor was watching and would come to Joshua's rescue. Let them find any tidbit of evidence, even the tiniest disproof that could cast enough doubt to delay a wrongful death. Seth silently pleaded.

Tomorrow morning's show, if there was an execution show, hopefully not, wouldn't include any segments of Joshua speaking live. Tonight was it. The executives at the network had agreed with Seth's opinion. They might show a few segments from tonight's broadcast or some footage of St. Edwards and Twin Falls City Park, but the decision had been made not to make the condemned young man speak as he walked to his platform of death…one small consolation.

Seth had not noticed before now how close the words 'executive' and 'executioner' were. They both had the same root and they both dealt in vile business.

Without the editing option, tonight's live show was becoming a total train wreck, but Seth didn't really care.

"Any last words, regrets, or anything you would like the world to know? This is your swan song moment."

Why had he added those last trite words, habit he supposed, he wished he could suck them back in, but Joshua did not appear offended.

"I have nothing to bequeath, so will leave my legacy in a short story… Like there are two falls in Twin Falls, in Israel there are two seas, the Sea of Galilee and the Dead Sea. Both are fed by the well-known Jordan River. One is teaming with life. Its waters contain twenty-seven species of fish, some found nowhere else in the world.

The shores surrounding it are blanketed by lush vegetation and birds. The other sea is toxic and bitter. No life lives there. They are both fed by the same source, so what makes the difference? The Sea of Galilee has a tributary of the river flowing from it, this sea shares its abundance. The Dead Sea hoards all its water with no outlet. So it is in life, if we only receive, but do not give, we do not live. I hope I have lived.

If there was anything else I could say that would make a difference in this world, I would say it. I choose to end by quoting another, far more elevated, innocent man whose words are much more powerful than mine and who is also my elder brother... *'Forgive them for they know not what they do'.*"

Seth leaned in towards his beloved younger brother, it was time, he knew he needed to finally reveal their related identity and ask for his own forgiveness in front of the world. But before Seth opened his mouth to speak, Bear the ultimate director, witnessing an untouchable ending, yelled cut and the screens of America's television viewing audience faded to black.

EPILOGUE

*Close the book now if you are satisfied and prefer an ambiguous ending.

What follows is an alternate ending for those who like things tied up in a pretty little package with no loose ends, to finish out their emotional ride with closure. If you would prefer to conclude the story in your own mind or determine what should happen yourself…please do not read.

3 MONTHS LATER:

The trio sat around the old apartment table looking out the back window over Lake Waxahachie. Boats skimmed the surface, some fishing, some skiing, across the six hundred acres of water. The surroundings were open and peaceful, totally the opposite of Seth's historic downtown living. He had moved almost a month ago now. Jonny and Amos did not follow him here as roomies, but finally felt able to move on to the next realm together. Joshua had moved with Seth to this new location on the lake and was sitting at the table with him and Halle. Much had transpired in the last three months since the execution. Seth was grateful every day that Josh was living with him, not as an apparition, but with real live flesh and blood.

After their intense Seth Row Special together, Seth decided not to whisper in Josh's ear their shared lineage, but waited until Father Brogan arrived the next morning. He gave the priest an opportunity to tell Joshua himself. If Sam did not, Seth assured his dad, he would. Seth did not want his brother going to the grave without knowing who he really was and that he had an actual family who loved and cared about him.

Humbled to the core, the man of cloth had taken the higher road. Real tears rolled down and splashed on his robes as Sam, with deep and apparently sincere sorrow, shared an abridged version of the story he had already told Seth. Joshua took the news better than Seth had and both sons were able to forgive their shared father. Staring death in the face from any angle does that to a person.

Sam T. Brogan promised to tell Eliza the truth too when he returned to Twin Falls. The girl, Joshua's twin sister, did not travel to the execution with the priest in hopes of keeping her identity safely hidden away from the media madness.

Seth and his crew had arrived, set up and were ready for the appalling live execution show to go on that fateful Saturday morning. It was to pre-empt the normal Saturday morning fare, ironically cartoons.

Less than an hour before air time, the governor's office called with a thirty day stay of execution to allow time to check out new leads on the case, those provided via Jonny, Halle, Seth and Bear.

A full pardon followed twenty-two days later, after DNA retrieved from Jonny's body matched Tom Truman's. Seth was sure Jonny had been there in Idaho helping along the official investigation. Truman it turned out was also the other anonymous phone caller on the show. Questioning Joshua's parenthood in hopes of creating mass hysteria about the boy in the Texas Bible belt as well.

Shortly following the conclusive evidence discovery, Joshua was released to Seth's custody. And Seth, a legal blood relative, was made his permanent guardian until Josh turned eighteen.

When Seth found out the good news, he impulsively asked Halle how she felt about having a teenage son, or twins, in a haphazard marriage proposal. It had come out of his mouth in jest, but after the words were given life, both had known they were right. Seth and Halle would be married as soon as all the final arrangements could be made. It would not be at the Bell Tower Chapel and Gardens as Tillie had planned, but a perfect place for the two of them….here on the lake in their own back yard.

Halle would be married, become a step-mom, and move in on the same day. It looked like their nuptials would probably take place before Bear and Ainsley's. When it was right, it was right. Bear would be his best man and then Seth would be Bear's a few weeks later. The two would be beginning another chapter of their lives together, but Seth was way ahead of him on the kid thing.

Tonight was a house warming for Seth, Josh, and soon to be Halle's, new home on Lake Waxahachie. The home was not ostentatious, but a perfect for them, three bedroom brick home with a dock and access to the lake. Water was soothing and cleansing. Seth and Halle hoped the waves would wash away much of the trauma Josh had experienced in his young life.

The guest list was small. Bear and Ainsley, Gun, Jake and Joey with plus ones, if they asked anyone. His mother and Raul were invited too and any paranormal beings who felt so inclined to join them.

Eliza Marie was flying into Love Field in Dallas in just three hours for the party and then planned to spend a few weeks in the third bedroom which would be designated hers. Eliza wanted to finish the postulate program first and find out if she felt called to take the vows of a nun. If not, Seth hoped she knew she would always have a place in his home…their home…his and Halle's. He liked the sound of that.

Marion would be at the house soon to help Halle with last minute food and set-up preparations, while Seth and Josh drove to pick up Eliza at the airport. His mother had been thrilled with their impending wedding plans and becoming a grandma so swiftly. Seth only hoped she would not want a double wedding, not his with Bear, but for herself and Raul. The couple was getting pretty chummy and were definitely headed in that direction, it was only a matter of time. Seth was pretty sure his father-in-law-to-be would shortly become his step-father as well. Seth was destined to go from no father, to four father figures in his life, if he added up all the titles.

Father Brogan would not be performing any of the ceremonies, not only were none of them Catholic, but Seth needed to keep some parts of his life separate. He did invite the priest as a guest and hoped he would come. This disjointed family all needed to share some therapeutic moments. Seth pitied the poor person who tried to figure out their family tree, it would look more like a tangled jungle. But it was good. He was happy. In the past year his family had gone from a mere two, he and his mom, to a soon-to-be seven, with more possible on the horizon.

The three were totally relaxed as they watched the smooth water wash in and out on their small strip of shoreline. Barney Fife was out back in doggy heaven, roaming around with his nose to the ground smelling the carpet of grass and dipping his paws in the water lapping the sand. Deputy dog had not stayed behind in the city, but made the rural move too.

"Interesting how calm the lake is right now, when it was so choppy just moments earlier." Halle observed breaking the silence.

"I choose smooth over rough water anytime...you know...for smooth sailing," Seth shared his life analogy opinion. "It feels delightful to float for a while, come up for air and not be buried by crashing waves."

"Smooth is nice Seth, but I like the mix, the choppy adds a taste of adventure and lets us appreciate the smooth. What do you think, Josh?" Halle asked.

The recently freed teen didn't answer for so long, the other two wondered if he had heard any of their conversation.

"Sorry, I was just appreciating the water and everything else. Savoring the moment I suppose. It still amazes me that I am here, sitting with you guys to see it. I never thought I would see anything else on this earth, besides the four cement walls with an iron barred door. I think I prefer water best flowing over me. Not drowning, but buried in the water, feeling it on every part of me, reminding me I am alive...like being baptized to my new life and beginning."

The surrogate parents had nothing to add to the wise words of their newly acquired son.

Instead Seth jumped up, "Let's go get our Sis."

AUTHORS NOTES

I woke up in the middle of the night with the title of this novel in my head knowing it was about a man who had a show about death row. The storyline and characters kept coming like they wanted to be told. Some made me laugh out loud. The unique premise made me uncomfortable at times throughout the process and the subject matter occasionally made me squirm. I hope I added light, or at least insights, to a dark topic.

All the facts about Waxahachie, The Rogers Hotel and Huntsville Prison are true, with one exception. Although the executions are done at the Huntsville Prison, the male and females on death row are both housed separately at prisons nearby. I made the locations the same for convenience of the story. I have a son and his family who live in Waxahachie, so have been able to visit this historical location on a few occasions and felt it would make an interesting setting for this book. Then I spent much of my youth growing up in Twin Falls, Idaho and am very familiar with that area. I attended concerts in Twin Falls City Park and had friends who attended St. Edwards Catholic School. It did not have a live-in facility during my lifetime, but I needed it to have one. The park is surrounded on the four sides by the structures and businesses mentioned.

I have not completely sorted out how I feel about the death penalty, but Seth and this story reflect part of my internal debate.

There is also a water theme subtly 'running' throughout the book. Water is life-giving, cleansing, healing, helps things grow, baptizes and is matter from which tears are made. It was not obvious, but there if you look for it…the name of one city is Twin Falls, also Shoshone Falls is there, higher than Niagara, the Snake River, rain falling, mud puddle, mist on shower, sweat, tears of many, drought (lack of water), hurricanes, floods, laps in a pool, submerged to the bottom, hot tub, sauna, Sea of Galilee, Dead Sea, Jordan River, moving onto the shores of Lake Waxahachie, etcetera.

Hopefully the reader will think about and feel things from different perspectives as they read the words of Seth Row. Blessings.

ACKNOWLEDEMENTS

I must give mounds of credit to the muses that surround me as I hike the hills of Mountain Green near Snow Basin Ski Resort in Utah. Most of whom I cannot see, but from which my mind receives impressions readily as I walk.

I also greatly appreciate my more human and huggable readers. My top teen-editor, who shares storyline input with me without pulling any punches, would have to be my oldest granddaughter, Halle Huber. Friends who also contributed to the ultimate outcome are Teri Sowby, Julie Hales and Sandy Ostler. They were all kind enough to give me insights as I wrote various drafts. Chelsea Buttars stoked my writing skills and was a believer in the project from day one.

Lastly, much gratitude to my son-in-law, Ryan Buttars, for designing Seth Row's eye-catching cover. He captured and rolled together the symbolism of prison bars, water theme, a subtle cross reference and the orange from the sunset outside reflecting the upcoming execution date Seth is racing against. Thank you all.

WORKS CITED:

https://en.wikipedia.org/wiki/Capital_punishment

https://deathpenaltyinfo.org/time-death-row

https://www.infoplease.com/us/crime/women-death-row-are-still-rare

Victor L. Streib's research in "Death Penalty For Female Offenders, January 1, 1973 through February 20, 2013."

http://cw33.com/2015/10/31/dfw-ghost-stories-haunted-history-a-permanent-guest-at-rogers-hotel/

http://blogforelliscountytexashistory.blogspot.com/2008/06/movies-filmed-in-waxahachie.html

https://www.balancedpolitics.org/death_penalty.htm

http://www.micheleknight.com/articles/psychic/psychic-readings/psychic-readings-explained/

http://deniselescano.com/psychic-readings/what-to-expect/

https://www.catholicidaho.org/clergy

http://listverse.com/2014/05/20/10-facts-you-might-not-know-about-death-row/

DISCUSSION QUESTIONS

1) What are your thoughts and feelings about the death penalty and our country's penal system in general?

2) What does Seth mean by the analogy that a man or woman becomes what they become "depending on which wolf they choose to feed"? Do you believe we create the person we are by the choices we make? Are you able to see both sides of the people whose path you cross? Or do you believe some people are just inherently evil and some good?

3) Could you or would you want to do Seth's job? Do you consider it worthwhile journalism? What do you think about the way media portrays events today? Do we need more good news?

4) What qualities did you especially like or dislike about Seth? What occurrences in his life contributed to the man he became?

5) Discuss and contrast Seth's three love interests….Junie Blue, Matilda Morgan and Halle Valentine. Which of the three did you relate to or like the best? Why?

6) Do you believe in paranormal happenings? Would you ever, under any circumstance, consult a psychic?

7) Did you think Joshua was a real person? Did you think he was guilty? Can a person really rise above the mundaneness of the world and have such an elevated view of life like Joshua did? How can that happen?

8) Did you think Seth was fair to his father? Did you find it ironic that a man needing forgiveness became a priest who could grant forgiveness in other people's lives but not his own? Do you think Seth should have forgiven him? How important is forgiveness in our lives?

9) What part did Marion play in the story? Is it interesting to ponder that every person born on this earth had a mother at some point? How much influence do mothers have?

10) Were you ever aware of the water theme running through the book? Are there any other themes you picked up on? What was the role of Barney Fife in the book?

11) Do you like an abrupt, cliff hanger ending or did you prefer the epilog with the "happily ever after" approach? How would you have ended the book?

12) Who would you cast to play the roles of these characters in Seth Row on the big screen? (Seth, Marion, Bear, Father Brogan, Halle Valentine and Joshua)

NEW NOVEL DEBUTING IN 2019

Not Really Homeless
By Teresa Meyerhoeffer Christensen

Poppy Paisley hails from a long matriarchal line who are all named after flowers. Since she has a permanent address at Greener Pastures, her Grandma Daisy's dementia care center, she does not really consider herself homeless. Even though she keeps her belongings in Sunny-mobile (her car) and sleeps at a different location each night. None of the people in her life are aware of her housing situation, except perhaps a park-dweller named Chet. He is her father-figure and the wisest person she knows. Poppy is studying to become a librarian and works at the public library with her best friend Russell and a butterfly aficionado. When a dashing library board member invites Poppy to help on a project that she has a vested interest in, she is able to confront her homelessness firsthand. Poppy rescues others along her journey, as she wrestles with the dilemmas of *what really makes a home* and *how does a person interpret reality*?

ABOUT the AUTHOR

Teresa Meyerhoeffer Christensen has experienced all the
elements of romance, drama, comedy, intrigue, tragedy
and adventure in over a half century of earth living. She
was born in Idaho to a basketball-playing, college
president father, and cheerleader mother, who taught her
to love to learn. She married her high school sweetheart,
graduated as an RN, battled cancer, raised six amazingly
unique children, taught institute and seminary religion
classes for years, was elected to the Bend-Lapine School
Board while living in Oregon and served on various
other boards in many volunteer positions, all while
writing in various capacities. Life is much quieter now
living up in Mountain Green and the veil between
heaven and earth, along with the air, much thinner. She
finally has time to put down on paper the many stories
that have been roaming around her head for years.
William Shakespeare was Teresa's 12th great uncle.